To Douglas & Mary

TOO LOVELY TO KILL

by

BOB ADAMS

lots of love

Bob

Published in 2011 by YouWriteOn Publishing

First Edition

British Library C.I.P.

A CIP catalogue record for this title is available from the British Library.

ISBN 978-1-908147-56-1

Cover Design by LIZZIE CAMERON

BOB ADAMS OBE

This is Bob Adams second novel. He has written and had performed and published several plays. His first play won him an Alan Ayckbourne prize for short, short plays in 1989. Since then he has written plays on conservation SCRAPPY, take over bids BANNOCK the BAKER, cloning HEBDEN(before it became a fashionable subject) and a comedy in a transplant ward in a hospital COMING APART. His latest plays, ABERDEEN ANGUS and THE ROUP, have been comedies set in the farming community.

His first novel SPYBUS was a humourous spy thriller.

Bob has worked in the timber and furniture industries in Africa and Scotland and has served as an officer in the Parachute Regiment. He has also been chairman of the Scottish Athletics Coaching Committee.

THIS is a tale of a normal, good humoured couple who inadvertently but not unwillingly get involved in a vicious drama.

Lance and Caroline Lockhart make friendly contact with a lovely red headed lady on their way to their holiday accommodation in Corsica. Lance notices on her luggage label that her name is Jean Faulds. They also learn that she is a police officer.

As they are dressing for their first dinner they hear a shot. On arriving at the dining chalet they find that there is another lady sitting in Jean's place. She introduces herself as Jean Faulds.

The Lockharts, having arranged to play tennis with the first Jean resolve to find out what is going on.

They phone a senior police officer who is a neighbour of theirs back home. He phones back and tells them that an important surveillance operation is underway and that Jean Faulds had indeed been replaced. A blood stained handkerchief confirmed that Jean one had been eliminated but nothing could be done about that until the operation was completed. He advised them to forget it and enjoy their holiday.

The Lockharts do not like the idea that Jean one's murder could so casually be put on the back burner so they struggle to find out what happened to Jean. Their natural good humour is sorely tested as they are drawn into the vicious activities of a ruthless smuggling gang.

Dedicated to Mary

TOO LOVELY TO KILL

CHAPTER ONE

The shot sounded near them.

'What was that?' A startled Caroline asked Lance.

'Gunshot.'

'I know that. But what for? Why?'

'Shooting little birds I should think. They like little birds.'

'Strange way of showing their affection.'

'To eat, darling. To eat.'

'Yuck!'

'Forget it. Complete quiet and tranquillity the hotel boasted. So I'm sure that will be the last shot we hear this holiday,' declared Lance, the opposite of prophetically.

'Bandits' his friends had warned when he told them of his holiday destination but Lance's first impressions of Corsica were entirely favourable. The caramel coloured crags soared into a cloudless blue sky, the temperature would have melted any caramels carelessly left out and the villages the bus passed through were quaint, picturesque and quiet; the locals lay in the sun or moved very slowly,

'Bandits - no chance,' He scoffed to himself and settled drowsily into the soft coach seat. Even when they stopped at a lovely stone built café and heard the gunshot no thought of villainy of any kind entered his mind.

He apologized as he proffered a large denomination note for two coffees. He felt less sorry about it when he saw the sum flashed up on the till. He reached for the change and was about to put it in his pocket when he was tapped on the shoulder.

'Count it,' instructed a quiet voice behind him.

He counted the notes nodded and again started to stuff the notes away.

'From the other end.'

Now irritated, Lance turned and saw that his advisor was a lovely lady with a luxurious head of golden red hair.

'Count the notes from the other end,' she repeated softly.

Shrugging his shoulders he did as she said. The count was a note less.

'One note is folded. Old trick.'

He found the doubled up note, smoothed it out and called the woman who had served him.

She brusquely dismissed his claim until the red head leant forward, looked the woman straight in the eyes and calmly shook her head. The bus driver, a rough looking character, pushed his way over to them and growled, 'Trouble, Michelle?'

The red head turned towards him and said sweetly but there was now a cold glint in her eye, 'No. But there will be soon - and I have a very loud voice.'

'It's all right, Bernard. I'll sort this out.' The embarrassed waitress turned away abruptly and returned with another note, apologizing, blaming the crowd and the hurry. The redhead again shook her head and the woman hurried off, red faced and flustered. Lance turned to thank his benefactor but she had gone over to a vacant chair and was sipping her coffee and chatting cheerfully to the couple sharing her table.

'Bandits' he growled in anguish as he pushed through the crowd to reach the table Caroline had secured in a shaded corner of the garden.

'Eleven euros and wrong changed' he barked as he banged down a cupful of dark liquid in front of her. 'No competition for miles. The bus only stops here between the airport and Villamaquis. The Office of Fair Trading should hear about this,' he complained loudly.

The couple nearest did not understand a word he was saying. But 'Tres bon,' responded a plump, beret wearing man lifting his cup in salutation.

A well dressed, alert looking man sipping an entirely different sort of beverage, smiled. This gentleman had been casting his eyes speculatively over Caroline, who looked good in her smart pale blue travel outfit. She was one of those trim women who do not seem to age. Four years younger than her husband she looked even more so; like a Felicity Kendal on aerobics.

The Frenchman frowned as Lance sat down and then, that possibility ended, swung his eyes around apparently seeking out other solitary ladies.

Lance noticed the man's interest but he had long since become used to the admiring glances directed towards his wife and his own ardent appreciation of her attractions lessened his resentment at the casting of covetous eyes on her; in fact it confirmed to him his own good fortune.

The Frenchman's roving eyes now rested on the tall, good looking red headed lady and gleamed. He rose and strolled as if to pass her, dropped a silk handkerchief by her feet, looked down as if seeing it for the first time, picked it up and offered it to her. She looked at it and shook her head emphatically and as the bus horn honked impatiently she stood up and strode past him without a glance. Lance was just enjoying the brush off and nodding his head in appreciation when he saw the bus driver embrace the proprietrix warmly, whisper to her and take from her a fat envelope before herding his sheep back into the bus. He stopped nodding and shook his head.

'That must be a month's commission,' whispered Caroline.

'At these prices! One day's,' growled Lance.

Lance took the two cups towards the bus and walked on past it and laid them on the wall at the point which would cause the café staff the longest possible walk. He felt a little better. Petty but better. Caroline looked at the boyish expression she had found so attractive in him when they first met and wondered if he would ever grow up.

The long red hair swung away from a pleasant, happy, sun kissed face as the girl who had noticed the doubled up note came alongside him. She was laughing at him. She reached the bus just as Lance did. He shrugged, smiled conspiratorially and made to give her his hand to assist her up the step but she sprung into the bus like a gazelle and, while he stood open mouthed as the long athletic, tanned legs passed his eyes, an older lady seized his hand, pulled herself up and thanks him profusely.

The road was tortuous and precipitous, the chunky, deeply tanned driver relaxed and confident and the passengers enthralled and apprehensive. Lance could occasionally catch glimpses of curves of golden sand tucked far below between the steep cliffs. The courier pointed out the places of especial interest and, in respect of the beaches, explained which were for the modest, which were topless and which were for the completely uninhibited; the Germans go there she explained.

Lance feigned a lack of interest in these beaches. The tall girl sat two seats in front. He noticed the long chestnut hair swing and bounce with the movement of the bus as it was thrown around the sharp bends and had to force from his mind the picture of such a girl on such a beach.

As if she were reading his mind, her relaxed laughter reached him followed by the laughter of the stranger fortunate enough to be sitting beside her.

The bus swung into a walled garden and pulled gently to a halt right beside a neat lawn. The bus driver turned, nodding as if smiling to his passengers but his mouth was hidden by a large rat shaped moustache and his eyes did not smile. He swaggered slowly towards the office block without a backward glance, a black battered brief case in his hand. He then turned and pointed in the direction of the bus as he spoke to someone in the shadows.

'He's pointing you out as a trouble maker.' whispered Caroline laughing.

Quietly, and with little fuss, those who had alighted were each allocated to a group of villas and informed where their respective dining chalets were. The bus driver returned and drove the remaining passengers to other areas. Lance noted with satisfaction that the young woman with red hair and bright eyes was to be with their group. She was dressed rather severely in a light grey suit with a white blouse which made Lance all the more enthusiastic about the prospect of seeing her more casually attired.

'Thank you for your help. I am too trusting.'

'I think she could tell that in your face.' She was mocking gently.

'Glad to see that you're with us.' Lance ventured. She smiled.

'Do you play tennis?' Lance continued.

He saw her glance at the tennis racket in her hand, raise an eyebrow cheekily, and look for a moment as if she might ask if he thought it was for catching butterflies, or words to that effect.

She didn't. Instead she said politely. 'I love the game. I'm not good but I am energetic.'

'Perhaps we can have a game?'

'Yes. I believe they organize competitions. That'll be fun. But I want to see the island too. I haven't been here before. Lots to do. That is a lovely suit your wife,' she paused briefly with a question in her eyes, 'is wearing. Very smart. Does she also play?'

'Oh yes. She's quite good.'

'Lovely. I look forward to seeing you both on the courts.' The friendly smile was swung towards Caroline to embrace her also.

'You look tired,' commented Lance sounding concerned. 'You look as if you need a day's rest before you start rushing around.'

'Thank you, I'm all right. I work hard.' As if to finish the conversation she thrust out her hand. 'Jean is my name.'

'Lance – and Caroline.'

It crossed his mind to offer to help with her luggage but when he saw Caroline struggling with hers he thought better of it. With a slight crinkling around her green eyes, the red head turned away. He watched her easy, loose stride as she made her way to her chalet thinking how beautifully she swung her long legs. He was still looking that way when she had gone from view.

'I play tennis too, remember,' remarked Caroline as they entered the colourful, pleasant rooms which were to be their home for the next two weeks.

'Just being friendly,' protested Lance while pulling and pushing at the drawers to pick one that slid easily. As a former furniture retailer nothing irritated him more than sticking drawers. To his delight the furniture was good quality; light, well polished wood with rattan inlay. It had a summer holiday look. He caressed the beautifully sanded corners.

'She'll be looking for a – friend somewhat nearer her own age, dear.'

'Mixed doubles. That's what I had in mind. Mixed doubles.'

'I'm pleased to hear it. She does seem a pleasant lass. I hope we can get a fourth. But just you be careful with her.'

'Why that?' asked Lance pulling his racket out of the case and swinging it viciously.

'Watch out, you great oaf. Because she's a police woman. That's why.'

'How do you know that?'

'Easy. The way she looks – that air of authority. The way she walks and the way she has her hair.'

Lance's mouth fell open as he looked at his wife.

'And,' she continued, 'I heard her talk to another policewoman at Heathrow. I think she'd found a stray child and was passing it on to be looked after. She seemed nice. The kiddie was reluctant to let her go. These big green eyes bewitch children as well is seems. She'll be a good mother some day, that lass. She told the other bobby she was off duty and going on holiday for a couple of weeks and was joking about what she would be doing while the other was pounding her hot feet across the hard airport floor,' Caroline continued. 'So I cunningly deduced that she was a policewoman.

Lance hit his bended wife smartly on the buttocks with his racquet.

'Your backhand's rubbish.' She laughed.

They had tucked away most of their things and Lance went out on to the verandah to enjoy the last of the sunshine and to get his bearings. Caroline joined him and threaded her hand into his. They said nothing. All was quiet.

Lance was just about to suggest they walk down through the garden for a cool drink when a sharp thumping sound broke the silence.

Lance grasped his chest in mock alarm and groaned, 'They've got me.'

'What was that?'

'A gun shot.' said Lance.

'Again. I'm not going to like it if they're going to shoot little birds near us.'

'I don't think that was shooting birds.'

'What do you know about – ? Sorry, I forgot. You're an expert. The Home Guard wasn't it?'

'Territorials. If that was a gun, the bullet didn't travel far.' He saw Caroline's troubled face and looking at his watch suggested, 'Let's get ready for food.' Then added firmly, 'Most likely a car backfiring.'

That evening as they sat down to dinner on a verandah overlooking the garden the red headed policewoman did not appear. There was one empty chair.

A dark haired, tanned, pleasant looking girl came out from the kitchen. 'Good evening. I am Meryl. Donna and I will be looking after you. I hope you all had a good journey and have a lovely holiday. I'm sure you will. If anything is not to your liking, please let us know immediately. Meantime I must leave you and see if the food is fit to eat yet. Do introduce yourselves and get acquainted. Won't be long.'

Meryl bustled in and out but was too busy to contribute much to the conversation. While the first course was being served another young woman, perhaps about thirty, came and sat in the vacant place. She introduced herself in a quiet English voice.

'Jean is my name, Jean Faulds.'

Seeing that she was sitting down in the seat he had assumed would be occupied by the lady who had saved him a Euro and who had definitely been allocated to this group, Lance started to ask, 'What happened to' -- but was cut short by a sharp kick from Caroline.

'The salt.' She finished his sentence and passed the salt. 'Here.'

Lance sprinkled the already salted food and spluttered as he took a mouthful. He looked at the late arrival. She was not going to add any glamour or, the admittedly out of reach, spice to the holiday that the redhead's presence had promised. The newcomer was of medium height and strong sturdy build. Her eyes were brown and unblinking. Her hair was black and cut severely short. She looked an outdoor woman; a woman of action. As if to avoid conversation she kept her head down over her plate. The meal was good and the evening passed pleasantly with the holiday makers telling something of themselves all hoping to start off their fortnight together in a friendly manner. There were two bright young men, Ian and Ross, who were obviously looking for sun, sport and female companionship; definitely not in that order. Jean Faulds listened in an absent way to the two young men but they seemed to be establishing very little in common with her; in fact she looked as if she found them boring. Kirsty, a serious faced lady in her mid thirties with wispy light brown hair and dressed in soft browns and greens, introduced herself quietly and declared that she hoped to climb and visit historic sites..

'Not rock climbing,' she explained. 'Just walking high in the hills. These mountains are a bit daunting. But I've been here before and I know you just have to find a stream and follow it and you're in a wooded paradise.'

'Alone?' asked Lance.

'Yes,' replied Kirsty, 'Unless you're volunteering?'

'I don't think my wife would let me go up into the woods with a pretty young girl,' jested Lance.

The homely young lady flushed.

A couple, old in their demeanour but with unlined faces, perhaps in their early forties, completed the group. They didn't say much but it was apparent from the frequent almost aggressive proclamations of his property and belongings that he was doing well, at what he didn't say except that he was a director, but his constant glances to see what others were doing and his slow care with his eating implements indicated that he was not used to the high life, even at this modest level. He was never first to start a course. Their holiday clothes had obviously never been worn before and Albert and Mabel Brodie had a pallor so deep that it made the other newly arrived sun seekers look tanned.

'The kick' asked Lance as they undressed. 'For why?'

'A policewoman on holiday doesn't want everyone to know what she is. And because something is not right. I feel it in my bones.'

'And such pretty bones,' remarked Lance looking appreciatively at his wife's still attractive body.

She hurriedly slipped on a brief nightgown – but not her specially bought holiday one. 'I want a night's sleep after that journey, so get that glint out of your eyes. And don't change the subject. That woman who sat down in place of our policewoman. There's something wrong.'

'You can tell by the way she eats?'

'Don't be sarcastic. Because her name is Jean Faulds.'

'So?'

'That was the name on our policewoman's luggage label.'

'You are so nosey, Caroline.' Lance was quiet for a moment. 'Why didn't you just let me ask her then?'

'I don't think that we should let her know that we're suspicious.'

'Are we suspicious?'

'Yes. We are. I didn't take to the newcomer.'

'Ah. Woman's intuition. Nor did I. She doesn't look like a tennis player.'

'And she's not so good looking.'

'Would I notice a thing like that when I have such a beautiful wife?'

'Why do you only say nice things to me when we're in bed? Well, I liked the original Jean too and I'm worried. Strange things happen in foreign places.'

'You mean white slaves.'

'Don't joke, Lance. I am sure there is an innocent explanation but I am a bit worried. And I don't want to worry all holiday. Listen, Lance let's find out. To set my mind at rest. You're good at puzzles. Crosswords and things. Let's find out what's going on. There's probably nothing to it but it'll be interesting to see what we can make of it. And I really am a bit worried. And intrigued.'

'Me too. I must say that if I were looking for a white slave she would be just right.'

'You have not to make fun of it.'

'Right, Lockhart and Lockhart public defectives. Yes, could be interesting.'

'And a little excitement. No dear - excitement starts tomorrow. Go back to your own side. We'll need clear heads in the morning.'

As Lance lay waiting for sleep to overtake him he turned over in his mind his expectations of this holiday. They had not been regular holiday takers; too busy. He thought of what had brought them to this place

Undoubtedly the stories he had heard of the Corsican sisters. The Corsican mountains are amongst the most beautiful in the world but they are inhospitable in the extreme, on the other hand, the Corsican sisters were not beautiful but their reputation for hospitality had spread far beyond the golden fringe of their adopted island home. Under the bare jagged peaks they had built a hostelry renowned for its food, its fun and its fair prices. Word of this gem among holiday retreats had even reach the ears of the Lockharts who had not hitherto travelled far.

Among its attractions for the more sophisticated of men and, perhaps even more so, for such women, was a total ban on children. For most people too old to have their family on holiday with them, too young to have started a family or just too careful, this was a powerful lure.

The low stone built cottages and the wild gardens had no swings or mini golf; the swimming pool had no chute and the catering included no toddlers portions of baked beans or burgers. The howls of spoiled children were not heard on the sand nor the whimper of unhappy children by the pool and, perhaps even more welcome, not even the screams, shouts and splashes of delighted happy offspring. Any screams or shouts were for other reasons. A calm prevailed but not a dullness.

CHAPTER TWO

Caroline was first to the breakfast table. The air was warm and still. The table was set on the verandah so she chose a seat facing out over the bay. No other buildings were visible. The villa was set half way up a hillside so that from where she sat she could only see dense clumps of trees and bushes to both sides, sloping lawns strewn with colourful shrubs in front and, further off, the calm turquoise sea. The soft sound of splashing and gentle laughter told of a pool a discreet distance from the chalet. A sleepy eyed man, still in evening attire, came out of a villa, and lurched uncertainly over the grass. A clattering sound started behind Caroline and a dark haired, tanned, pleasant looking lass dressed in a minimal blouse, which displayed her rounded bosom to maximum advantage, and a colourful skirt come out from the kitchen which backed onto the verandah and laid out glasses and jugs of fruit juices.

'Bonjour mademoiselle. C'est tres jolie.' Caroline ventured in her rusty French.

'Good morning. I am Donna. You have met Meryl. She and I will be looking after you. I hope you slept well.'

'Oh, you're English. That'll make life easier - although I was hoping to brush up my French.'

'You'll get lots of that.' said Donna. 'But you'll find the accent difficult.'

Mabel Brodie arrived next, carefully chose two shaded places, selected cereals and placed one bowl in front of the chair she was reserving for her husband. With her head down she munched away bovinely. She was even dressed in cow colours, soft browns and creams, and her eyes were round and gentle. Then Lance arrived, picked up a juice and dumped himself down beside Caroline. He looked as if he were bursting to say something but Caroline glowered him into silence. He was closely following by Kirsty breathing heavily having, as she explained, gone to the top of the hill to see what lay on the other side. 'More hills' she replied to the obvious question. 'But very beautiful.'

The young men lurched in, heavy eyed with sleep, and consumed mountains of cereal and fruit. They laughingly teased each other about their relative prospects for the holiday and discussed a visit to the water sports centre. Last to arrive was Albert Brodie.

'Well, did you see it?' hissed his wife in an angry whisper her soft face flushed.

Brodie shook his head. 'No.'

'Well, forget it now. We're on holiday.' She whispered, her shoulders twitching as they were to learn they always did when her husband spoke.

'Settled in?' asked Lance.

Brodie looked up to see that everyone was listening. 'Very well thank you. Rooms a little poky when you are used to a bit of space. But for holiday accommodation - not bad at all.' His wife twitched and frowned at him.

Now that they were all present Donna explained that she and Meryl would alternate for breakfast but they would both prepare and serve dinner each evening and would join the guests for that meal.

'Very informal,' she said, 'and friendly - I hope.'

Caroline turned to Lance as soon as they got back to their villa.

'Right, spill it out. What's getting you so excited?'

'You for a start. My eyes are reaching parts I don't see the rest of the year. But apart from that -- ssh -- listen.'

The Brodies were passing the window and they could just hear the angry whisper again. 'Forget the body. It's not important.'

Albert resigned response was not audible.

Caroline shivered in spite of the heat. 'A body' she repeated, wide eyed. She sat heavily on the bed. 'You were saying, Lance?'

'Well, I can't top that - but I have spied out that Jean Faulds two has Jean Faulds one's luggage in her chalet. Including the tennis racket. Am I allowed to ask her if she plays? That would be harmless and if she says no - well.'

'It would add to our suspicions, not much more. But the body. I don't like the sound of that. Something horrid has happened, Lance. Where has our red head disappeared to? And I don't like the look of Albert.'

'Let's go down to reception. Ears to the ground. Meet the Sisters. They must be a lovely pair to run a place like this. Hear what's going on.

I'm still sure there's a simple explanation for all this. Let's leave the magnifying glass and finger print powder and take our costumes and towels and try to look like normal holiday makers.'

'You'll have to take that ferret like look off your face. Right, let's go. I'm worried about Jean one now.'

'Yes, me too. But I've been thinking about it. Let's not be silly. There is either a simple explanation or it's too serious for us to fool around. Let's discuss the whole thing with the sisters.'

With this resolution they relaxed.

They had some difficulty getting access to the Corsican Sisters, as everyone in the compound called them; obviously they believed in delegation. When they eventually entered the office they unrelaxed again. The two ladies sat facing them from the other side of a giant desk. They were large ladies with strong faces, prominent noses, dark haired and tanned. They were both dressed almost completely in white. Neither wore rings but the plumper one had a colourful bracelet of a type they were to see often in the local shops. Lance guessed they straddled forty with the larger being the younger. They had broad welcoming smiles but there was a toughness and business like authority about their pronouncements. Four large hands lay on the desk in front of them.

Lance apologised for disturbing them but the sisters acknowledged that they were there to cater for the customer's every need and desire. To their surprise when they were thus addressed the speech and accent were again English. They smiled sweetly at Lance as he started to explain their worry about the missing Jean Faulds. The smiles became less cordial as he expressed his fears. Their response was the equivalent of a shrug of the shoulders.

'But you must enquire.' insisted Caroline.

The sisters glanced at each as if deciding who should speak. 'No indeed we must not.' said the older one in a low growl her eyes narrowing 'We promise our clients utmost discretion. They can do what they like as long as they don't upset other guests. If they wish to swap around so be it. In fact we don't want to know. Nor do we encourage other holiday makers to concern themselves with matters which are really none of their business. Utmost discretion. This is a place for romance and frivolity. Our only difficulty is the temptation for members of the staff to get involved. We do not, of course, tolerate that.' She frowned at her sister.

'So I suggest, in fact I insist, that you forget this and enjoy yourself. That, after all, is what you are here for - and what we are here for.'

'But the first Jean Faulds was --,' Another perfectly timed blow stopped Lance in mid flow.

'Going to play tennis with us,' continued Caroline.

'Perhaps this lady also plays. Anyway there is not usually much difficulty is getting partners. You will obviously prefer doubles now.' The younger sister seemed to wish to be pleasant.

Lance frowned.

The slimmer sister continued. 'Now, if you don't mind we have a lot to do. You would be surprised how much has to be done to keep this resort informal. We have to organise quietly, almost secretly. You won't see much of us but I am sure you will feel our presence. Now we must get on. If you wish to go the village the mini bus leaves in fifteen minutes. Do enjoy yourself. You will find our staff most helpful but if you have an important matter,' (It was clear she did not consider the present discussion as such.) 'I am Mona and my sister is Rhoda.'

'And don't worry,' added Rhoda in an attempt to be placatory, 'we have instances where we don't hear anything ever again of someone who has checked in. We have fun exchanging speculations as to where they have gone. We usually come up with a romantic theory.' They smiled at each other.

'It is also the reason why we like to be paid in advance.' They both laughed as if this were a great joke.

Out in the poolside sunshine before they could think of anything else to say Lance and Caroline felt compelled to buy drinks and look as if they were indeed enjoying themselves. They stretched out on loungers and sipped at the unwanted drinks looking guiltily over to the office.

'She's right of course. It is none of our business. She probably has done some kind of swap with someone. They do nowadays - I believe. Better not to think about it.'

Lance was quiet for a bit. 'I don't think so - not Jean one.'

'What makes you say that?'

Lance again hesitated before speaking. 'She wasn't that sort of girl.'

'That remark is at least twenty years out of date.'

'And she sounded as if she was looking forward to playing tennis with me - us. She really did. I can tell.'

'I'm sure you can. Did anyone ever tell you that you have a big head? What could a young girl like that see in an old retired man like you?'

'Early retirement - so you can forget the old. And she wasn't a girl she was a woman.'

'Well, there was still a gap that nothing you have could bridge.'

'Very droll. And why the kick again? I don't have trousers on. I'm beginning to look as if I have been playing against Leeds United.'

'I had a feeling that the revelation that Jean one was a policewoman would have set these cats among the pigeons. I didn't like the stress on secrecy. Who is hiding what? I'm getting more and more worried. Do they know more than they said? They sounded conspiratorial.' Caroline looked hard at Lance. 'Do you feel reassured?'

Lance's face crumpled. 'No, I must admit I do not. Can we phone someone in Britain and find out about Jean one? If she is really is in some branch of the police it shouldn't be too difficult to find out.'

'And if she is having a little saucy sex we will be very popular.'

'True - but we'll have to take that chance. I hate doing nothing. I still have that feeling in my bones. I won't be able to relax and enjoy the holiday until we know she is all right. And the mention of a body. Makes my blood creep. Talking of which – look, there go the Brodies. They're making for the mini bus. Let's go too.'

Albert and Mabel were walking slowly in the direction of the bus. They could now see that Albert was much taller than Mabel and strode so that he was always half a pace ahead of her. She wore a constant expression of annoyance - maybe for that reason. Lance took hold of Caroline and hurried round the back of the offices. As she protested he explained that if they hurried they would get on the bus first so it wouldn't look as if they had followed the other couple aboard.

'You've been reading too many detective stories.' she protested.

When they reached the bus Kirsty was aboard quietly conspicuous amid a brightly clad mixture from other villas. "Like the inside of a bag of liquorice allsorts," thought Lance. There were two pairs of seats left. Caroline made for the front one but Lance pulled her into the rear seat and the Brodies settled down in front of them. Caroline shot an appreciative glance at Lance.

'Back with the sisters you didn't mention Brodies' body', whispered Caroline.

Lance looked at the man in front. 'I can't think of anything to say about it. To say it was just an ordinary body would be to flatter it.'

'No, you fool. The body he spoke of. You didn't say anything to the sisters.'

'I was beginning to feel just a little foolish without that. Let's wait and see if we can learn a bit more before we say anything else.'

'Nor did you mention the shot.'

'For the same reason. And we agreed it almost certainly wasn't a shot.'

They sat quiet and listened. The Brodies said nothing until they were almost in the village square.

Then Mabel spoke. 'If you're set on going I'm not coming. You're morbid you are.'

'Part of the job.' mumbled Albert. 'I'll meet you at the Patisserie at half past twelve. O K?' Mabel nodded mutely and they climbed out of the bus and went their separate ways.

'Did you hear that? He's off to do something morbid. It's this body again. I don't like the sound of this – or of him.'

'I'll follow him,' said Lance. 'Off you go to the beach.'

'Don't be daft. Look at you.'

Lance was wearing a multi coloured shirt and lurid blue shorts. He looked at Caroline's pale beige trouser suit and saw the power of her unspoken argument.

Caroline smiled triumphantly. 'See you at that wine bar about twelve thirty. Probably sooner.'

'Well, just to observe. Don't do anything daft. Just find out where he goes. And be careful, darling.'

'You too, sweetheart. Keep your hat on. The sun is very strong.'

Lance snorted and turned away. Caroline hastened after the receding figure of Albert who was shambling off along the coast road. Lance went into a newspaper shop, bought nothing, started to walk along the shore then returned to the paper shop, bought a local paper and tried to see if there was any police report which would explain the alluded to body. Nothing. As he sat in the shade he thought of the beautiful red head.

Now alone, without Caroline to rationalise for him he had the overwhelming feeling that something dreadful had happened to her and he felt miserable.

He got up and paced energetically about the sea front – not even paying attention to the half naked girls frolicking on the sands.

Perhaps she's dead, he thought and then he remembered that Caroline was tracking a man they knew nothing about; a man who might have been involved in a killing.

CHAPTER THREE

Caroline had no difficulty in following Albert as the earnest man showed no sign that he feared a follower. His white shirt and black trousers caused him to stand out both from the peacock tourists and the rustic locals. He never once glanced back and his only indecision seemed to be in finding his own way. He referred to a bright new guide book frequently. After he had gone three quarters of a mile he turned off the coast road and started up a steady incline. Caroline was now having to stride out and was irritated to see dark moist patches appearing on her lovely new suit. She kept to the shady side of the paved way for a time but decided this made her look too surreptitious so, cursing the sun, the man and the body, she strode on in the open.

To Caroline's relief Brodie, apparently feeling the pace and the heat, slowed down for a time then he seemed to see something that caused him to quicken again. Caroline rounded a corner and saw no Albert. A huge gate, narrowly open, was visible and led through to some great, gloomy Cypress trees. There was nowhere else he could have gone so in she squeezed. Now abandoning all pretence that she was out for a normal stroll she crept forward from tree to tree trying to catch a glimpse of Brodie. There was a rough track, infrequently used by the look of it, leading up through the dark trees. Caroline kept close to the trees and darted forward between them. For several minutes she kept this up feeling increasingly foolish and irritated. She came at last to a shady clearing. A figure loomed right in front of her. Her breath lumped in her throat and stifled her scream. She stood as still as stone. As did the figure - with better reason. She saw she had almost bumped into a crumbling angelic statue. She tried, unsuccessfully, to laugh, looked past the half fallen angel, saw another and realised she was in some sort of graveyard. As she turned to flee, Lance's scornful face flashed in her mind. She bit her lip turned back and pushed on through the undergrowth.

The clearing now opened out into a rough roadway. She crept forward to the junction and saw a row of lovely holiday chalets. She chuckled and strode forward.

They were beautiful small buildings in local stone, some with black and white checkered roofs, some with large windows and many with neat gardens. She approached one to see if there was any indication of the occupier. There was - an elaborate, ornate inscription plate; name and final tribute. On top of each roof stood a stone cross. She shivered in the hot sun as she realised that she was still among the crypts. The bright little sepulchres stretched in all directions. Of Albert she could see nothing. The quiet filled her with dread. She longed to hear a bird or the splash of the sea. But no - dead silence. 'Dead!' she shuddered. Then she decided if she could stay silent amidst all this she would surely hear Brodie. She held her breath. She could not restrain her thumping heart.

A bird did come to keep her company but it was a huge black ugly crow. It fitted the sombre scene perfectly. It too kept quiet and fixed its eyes directly on one particular secluded crypt. Peering in that direction Caroline saw fresh tracks through the unkempt path. They seemed to lead back towards a less overgrown way which however still did not seem broad enough for a vehicle. Cramp started to worry her as she stood awkwardly still and she dreaded that her bones would make a give away creak if she moved in the slightest. After an interminable wait there came a scuffling noise from the crow's crypt and out came Brodie blinking but looking bright eyed and with a hint of a smile. He glanced left and right then strode off and almost loped up some steep steps in the direction of the broader path.

Caroline stretched herself, nodded appreciatively to the crow which took fright, spread its ragged wings and flew off. She sauntered with a nonchalant air past the crypt. A light temporary door was closed but arcs scratched on the dry ground showed where it had been opened. Taking a deep breath, and persuading herself that having come this far -- , she stepped forward and pulled at the door. She had to tug as hard as she was able to get it sufficiently ajar to squeeze through. Inside it was dark but the sun was right behind her so a strong beam of dusty sunlight shone straight in. As her eyes adjusted to the gloom she saw a bright new coffin set on a black marble plinth. She stood nervous, bewildered and embarrassed for a minute then curtseying awkwardly she backed out of the crypt, carefully avoided stepping in a large pool of congealing blood; red highlights picked out by the shafts of sunlight. She squeezed out, pushed shut the door and stepped out into the bright day.

As her eyes adjusted to the brightness she thought she saw half of a face looking towards her from a tree far up the hill. She blinked her eyes and looked again. It was gone. She fled past more monuments, graves and little buildings and rushed back to Lance.

Lance looked up alarmed as Caroline hurried into the wine bar.

'Darling, you look as if you've seen a ghost. I got that wine for you but I think a spot of brandy in it would be welcome. Right? Sit here and I'll get it.' He brought the brandy across as she shivered in the warm room. 'Well,' he asked, 'Interesting?'

Caroline took the brandy and gulped. Lance looked in amazement. Caroline was not a drink gulper. She did not speak.

'Right,' said Lance, 'Let me tell you what I've been up to while you've been enjoying yourself.'

He started to recount his morning's activity. He had met Jean Faulds two on the promenade and had exchanged pleasantries with her but learned nothing. It then occurred to him that he had time to pass and could perhaps use it to 'pursue their enquiries'. He caught the little bus back to the villa explaining to the driver that he had forgotten his sun glasses. As he hoped, a strange girl was walking between the chalets. She was dressed like a holiday maker but had a small apron on. He waited till she was beside chalet six then approached her.

'Good morning. Lovely morning. I was looking for Meryl or Donna. Are they about?'

'Good morning, sir. No. I haven't seen them lately. Can I help you?'

'Just trying to get my bearings. I'm Lance Lockhart. I've left my sun glasses. Mind if I pop in and get them? Wife must have the key.'

The girl opened the door and beckoned him past her. 'You can both have a key. Ask at the reception.'

As soon as he was in the room he shot over to the luggage rack and tore a small piece off a label. He came out again as quickly as he could.

'Miss.' He shouted after the girl who had only gone a few paces. 'Sorry this is not our chalet. Ours must be four.' He pointed. 'That one I think.'

'That is number four. I'd better come and check. They all look alike. If this isn't it we'll check on the chart in the kitchen.'

It was, of course, the right chalet and the girl went off about her chores as Lance strolled down the hill for exercise and to fill in time.

'I could get used to this,' said Lance sipping his wine appreciatively. 'I know now why some criminals do it for the thrill. The old heart was beating away and I was only telling a little lie. Quite stimulating in a way.'

'Why?'

'Why what?'

'I could understand your sneaking into Jean Faulds One's room but not Jean Faulds Two. What did you get out of that? Not a big thrill I wouldn't think.'

'This.' Lance made a great play of looking round the busy bar to make sure no one was watching then slapped the small scrap of paper, with a triumphant flourish, on the table.

Caroline picked it up turned it over twice the read out 'ton' then 'kshire.' 'I hope you didn't put yourself in great danger to get this.' She flicked it back at him.

'Don't you see dear? That label must have been written by Jean One. At the courtesy bar you help yourself to drinks and sign your name. We'll be able to compare the writing. It might be a little step forward. See if the person who says she is Jean Faulds wrote the label. I don't see quite where it gets us but it seemed better than sitting here worrying about you.'

'Were you worrying about me? How nice. Well, you had cause to I can tell you. I was scared out of my wits. I don't think I like this game.'

'Tell me about it.'

'For another brandy.'

Caroline accepted the second glass then settled down and told Lance exactly what had happened with only the occasional dramatic embellishment.

'But the crypt looked like I think crypts should look and the coffin looked like any other coffin. If it hadn't been for the strange expression on Brodie's face I would say a normal local burial has taken place and they will now seal up the crypt till the next family bereavement. There were even fresh flowers.'

'Normal local burial.' Then with a resigned tone to his voice Lance asked, 'You didn't by any chance notice the name on the coffin?'

'No, I did not notice the name by chance. I very carefully and at extreme cost to my nerves read it. It was Fournier.'

'And the Christian name?'

'You're joking. And double my time in there. No chance.'

He patted her hand. 'Well done, dear. We'll look in the obituaries for a Fournier.'

He searched the paper, found the appropriate column and then proclaimed. 'There is. Look. Jacques Fournier. He died three days ago. That must have been him.'

'Well, I hope he forgives my intrusion. You know this is getting past a joke. Let's forget this nonsense, behave like adults and enjoy our holiday. I've had my adventure. I may even have enjoyed it in a strange way. It was all rather beautiful in fact. But wet blood. I think seeing that made me realise what it was all about. That upset me.'

'You may be right,' responded Lance but he sounded disappointed.

They walked around the delightful village, mentally registered some local craft products which might merit further consideration, had a coffee at a quaint old converted fisherman's shack, full of stuffed fish, floats and flotsam. They hadn't yet seen anything of the village so, as they had heard at breakfast of an interesting feast day procession due to pass soon, they had a stroll in the direction of the main avenue.

In spite of a firm resolution to the contrary they were tempted to stop for a light lunch by the fragrance drifting from a dark doorway and by the chance to give their hot feet a rest. A steaming tureen of the local fish soup was set before them and they kept refilling their bowls with the tasty brew.

Refreshed, they walked again. A brass band could be heard in the distance. They walked towards the music and were soon rewarded with a most colourful spectacle. The first few floats were of biblical scenes; some solemn and manned by adults, others more cheerful with happy smiling children delighted to be up on a lorry and the centre of attention. Towards the end of the procession a few of the floats seemed dedicated to more recent icons. They included a colourful presentation of Snow White and the Seven dwarfs with fat, jolly, bearded infants. At least there were six jolly bearded infants and one tearful, reluctant dwarf.

'In accordance with the way of the world, I reckon that one is Happy,' laughed Lance.

This was followed by a stately tableau of a beautiful Sleeping Beauty attended by an anxious looking Prince Charming. The next one was on a Rambo theme so Caroline decided that was enough of that.

They returned to the bus tired and a little more relaxed. Albert and Mabel were sitting across the aisle.

Lance slumped in the soft seat as the little bus bounced up the road then he shot upright.   'Blood you said?' Lance's sharp voice broke Caroline's reverie. 'Surely corpses don't bleed after three days?'

Caroline shuddered. 'Ssshh. No, that doesn't seem right. But don't talk about that here. Must have been -- I don't know. Anyway, not another word till we're in the chalet.'

Lance was about to respond when they heard Albert say quietly but clearly spreading out his arms as he spoke. 'But blood.'

CHAPTER FOUR

'Blood! A vanishing lady is one thing but blood and a body - that's too much. We must tell the police.'

'In French. Oh Lord.' Lance forehead puckered. 'Why does Albert always talk so loudly if he has something to hide?'

'A little deaf maybe. Deaf people don't realise they're talking loudly.'

'Well, his wife always seems to want him to shut up.'

'So what's different? But blood. Oh, Lance let's phone Lawrence. If Jean One is a British policewoman a man in his position must be able to find out something.'

'He'll laugh'

They trekked once more to the village having decided against risking the resort phone. Lawrence did not laugh; Chief Constables are not often the laughing kind and he regarded Lance and Caroline as a sound and sober couple. Neighbours who had become friends and with whom he and his wife dined from time to time. He promised simply, without betraying any emotion or opinion, that he would make enquiries and asked them to phone again the following morning. He made no response to Caroline's plea for discretion.

They hurried back up hill as the light faded.

'This would be quite romantic at half this pace.' complained Caroline glancing back at the moonlit sea. She looked longingly at two convenient stone seats.

'We mustn't be late for dinner. Not courteous.'

'And you might miss something.'

They showered quickly but were last to reach the table and the buzz of voices was already rising. Meryl and Donna obviously saw as part of their duties the lubricating of the conversation. They eased this task by keeping topping up the glasses with the local wine which was included, without limit, in the cost of the holiday. The sky was now deepest aquamarine and the lights were directed only on to the table and a few of the more attractive trees. Blood and bodies slid into the background as they settled down amongst the friendly group.

Kirsty was quietly but enthusiastically talking of her day. She had taken a local bus to an ancient historical site and was lyrical about the experience.

'The stones were eight thousand years old. Looked like a graveyard.' Lance and Caroline exchanged glances and groaned as the body came back to centre stage in their minds. 'Or they may just have been monuments of some kind.'

'Where is this?' asked Brodie. 'Sounds interesting.'

'Filitosa. About fifteen miles away. A bus goes past it twice a day. I recommend it. Masses of lovely wild flowers. Look, here's a leaflet.'

She held out a small coloured leaflet and Ross took it. He looked at it silently then turned to Donna. 'Can you translate this caption for me?' He read slowly from the pamphlet. 'Statue-menhir Filitosa 111 de dos. Symbole phallique?'

As Ian snatched the leaflet, looked at the photograph and chortled. Donna retorted that he could work it out for himself.

Kirsty tried to recover the paper as it passed quickly round the sniggering group. Eventually she got her hands on it and stuffed it in her pocket.

'Anyway they were most impressive.' She blurted out defiantly.

'If you like that sort of thing,' added Ian.

Lance was trying to think of a way of getting the girl off the hook when Brodie interrupted in a serious voice. 'They must have found some bodies.'

Lance and Caroline exchanged glances again and Lance croaked, 'Why that?'

'It mentions dates. Best way to tell the age of monuments and artifacts. A body is like a book if you know how to read it.'

'I prefer a talking one myself,' said Lance.

'They didn't have talking books when I was young.' Caroline turned away from Albert to discourage his continued contribution to the discussion.

'They wouldn't have got a word in,' quipped Lance.

'Sweet,' cut in Meryl deliberately. 'We have profiteroles or our fifteen flavour fresh fruit salad.'

'How can you say that without f-f-faltering?' stuttered Ian.

While they busied themselves on the important matter of

nourishing themselves Caroline listened carefully to the conversations around hoping to pick up - she didn't know what.

'Have you ever wind surfed?' Ross asked Ian.

'Tried once. A premature precipitation you might have called it. I wouldn't mind having another go.'

'Let's try tomorrow. If the sea is calm.'

'Yes. All we need is a dead calm sea and a brisk wind.'

Caroline decided this conversation was not going to help in their enquiries so she switched her attention to Meryl who was answering questions on the local attractions. She was very fair haired which made her look even more tanned than Donna. Her low cut dress also revealed a lot of brown skin but on a body much slimmer than that of Meryl. She was explaining that she and Donna worked in chalets in the Alps in the winter and came here for the summer. This was her third summer as against Donna's second so she knew the area well. She was very enthusiastic about the resort and spoke highly of the Sisters organisation.

'You don't often see them but you feel their presence. I don't think anything could go wrong without them knowing. They're sweet but heaven help you if you cross them. When they fall out with a local you don't even see him around the town after that.'

'Quite right too,' said Jean two pulling at her short dark hair.. 'They've got a wonderful place here. They mustn't let anyone spoil it for them - or us.'

'Do you play tennis, Jean?' asked Lance swinging his leg out of range of Caroline.

'I'm learning.' answered Jean with a tentative smile. 'I hope there will be a beginners' competition.'

'Enter the mixed. They will give you a reasonable partner I'm sure.' said Donna.

'Do either of you two lovely ladies play?' asked Ross of Meryl and Donna ignoring the opportunity to volunteer to partner the stern Jean.

'Depends on work load.'

'My husband is quite strong and he likes a change of partner.' Caroline turned back to face Jean. 'Don't you dear. And he's good at telling you exactly where to go.' She beamed at Lance.

'That's very nice of you - him. But I do want to explore the countryside - so we'll see.' Jean two rose from the table, excused herself and disappeared out of the circle of light.

'So that if she's up to anything you'll be able to get close to her - get under her defences.' As she brushed her teeth Caroline answered Lance's indignant protest about being volunteered to partner Jean Two.

'You didn't say that about the red head. Get under her defences. Oh, I shouldn't be joking about her. She might be - .'

Caroline climbed into bed. 'Don't even think about it until we hear from Lawrence. Come over here and forget all about it.' She had her holiday night dress on.

But later on she cried herself to sleep as she thought of what might have happened to the lovely girl.

They ate a quick breakfast before the others were up and hurried down to phone Lawrence from a box in the village and found him in serious mood.

'There is something going on. Our people were not too pleased to hear that your suspicions have been aroused. They know Jean Faulds has gone missing almost as soon as she arrived. Your mention of the shot has worried them. They had already instructed her contact to take her place. They are not sure yet if this was a good idea. A bit dicey but no choice really. However Judy, Jean to you now, is evidently a first class and experienced officer. A tough little lady. She has apparently already sent a package back here but that will be no concern of yours. They will let Judy – Jean know if it is something to be followed up. You are to tell her all you know and anything more you find out - but they don't want you interfering. This is an important and delicate surveillance operation, coming to a head soon. One clumsy move and a year's work is up the spout. So, no clever stuff. Tell the policewoman all you know especially about this bloody body. That's worrying our people. Phone me again tomorrow. But don't tell anyone you are going to do so. I'll perhaps have more by then. And, I am told no mobile phones or emails to be used on this piece of action. Not secure. As the world is finding out. So remember that. And keep any messages vague and brief. But unless she specifically asks for your help, which I'm sure she won't, forget it and have a good holiday. Even your new friend, who I hear is a smart operator, is not allowed to report back. Anyway look after yourselves and have a great time. Bring Caroline round to dinner when you get back. And I repeat. Don't interfere. Just a minor hiccup. Meantime enjoy the sun. You lucky blighters.'

They strolled to the wine bar, were tempted but decided to forego the brandy, and sipped a glass of cold, dry wine.

'I don't like being ordered not to interfere,' complained Lance.

'And I don't like the possible death of a young lady being described as a minor hiccup.'

'Nor me.'

'Listen, Lance. We're involved whether we like it or not. We talked to the girl. We heard the shot. If it was a shot. And we seem to be the only ones who care what happened to her. So, let's find out. As we agreed you are good at puzzles. This is more important than your crossword. Let's find out what's going on. You said you wanted some excitement now you're retired. Some adventure. Remember you wanted to run away and join the Foreign Legion once?'

'That was when I was sold that job lot of teak furniture as Jacobean. I was young. That deal nearly ruined me before I was properly started. And I wasn't married to you then. You are adventure enough. But I must admit I wouldn't mind a bit of excitement.'

'Well, this is it. There's probably a simple explanation but it will be interesting to see what we can make of it. Why would she disappear like that? If someone had to take her place right away she must have been doing something important. And if she is a British policeman we have a duty to do what we can for her. If it is not too late. I really am worried – intrigued as well.'

'Nosey. I said so. But I agree. Right Lockhart and Lockhart on the trail. Sounds good. Yes, it will add a bit of variety to the vacation. And keep your fair face out of the freckle front.' Lance was trying hard not to sound as worried as Caroline.

'Well, I certainly don't want to spend all my holiday lying on the beach. And we might just find out something useful. No one else seems to be bothering their bottom.'

'Surveillance,' Lawrence said. 'That means smuggling. Almost certainly. Which in turn that means arms or drugs. Nothing else matters now. I've heard that drugs move about these mountains.'

Caroline looked up at the immense mountains with their bright crags and deep shadowed fissures. 'They couldn't have picked a better place. You could hide an army up there.'

'That's why the seaside and the ports are watched. It's when they try to move the stuff out or in that they're vulnerable. We'll have to pick our time and place to contact Judy - no better stick to calling her Jean even between ourselves, daren't slip up. I'm glad she's on our side. She looks a tough nut.'

'Why don't you offer her a tennis lesson. Now you're on the same side you won't have difficulty with her defences. And if she does offer to show her gratitude in any tangible form tell her that Lawrence has told you to keep away - and so have I. These strong silent types are often very sexy. Seriously - make the offer but if she declines you will still have to go ahead and tell her what we know. She should be alerted that Albert wants watching.'

It was late afternoon when Lance made contact with Jean Two. She was coming out of the office, dressed as if she had been out walking. She was heading briskly towards her chalet when he intercepted her.

'Ah, Jean. I was looking for you. Fancy a knock up on the courts? Loosen up for the tournament. Caroline has a headache so I'm looking for someone to hit a few with.'

Jean looked surprised and not too pleased. 'No sorry. I have something - I'm not in the mood. But thanks. Maybe another day.'

Lance put on his most charming smile. 'Well, how about just sitting by the trees and having a glass of wine? Lovely time of the day.'

'No, thank you. I am even less in the mood for that.'

'No. No. Wait, I know you must be very busy.'

'Busy? What do you mean busy? I'm on holiday.' She frowned.

'Relax. I know about you. I've got some information for you.'

Jean looked closely at Lance as if making up her mind what to think. 'Right, bring an orange juice over there. This had better be good.'

As he ordered the drinks Lance rehearsed how he could explain the position to Jean Two without sounding foolish. She looked very warily at him as he approached and he formed the distinct impression that she had a weapon available and would use it if need be. As he was about to start they heard the voice of one of the sisters giving a mild roasting to Donna who was reporting the breakage of four cups, the loss of a sheet and a kettle, and a broken recliner. They heard the sister promise instant action on the breakages and was starting into her rebuke on the losses when Jean frowned and suggested they move.

'If we can hear them they can hear us.'

They moved and Lance got right to the point. 'I've talked to the police.'

She gasped. 'You've what?' She looked apprehensive.

'It's O K. They've told me you're all right. They're worried about Jean Faulds but they say they have confidence that you will do all that can be done.'

'I'm pleased to hear that.' She relaxed a little. 'I think you'd better tell me the whole story. Quietly.'

Lance talked in a low voice for a long time trying to be matter of fact yet making sure that she appreciated that they had been right to be concerned. Jean listened carefully, nodding knowingly at times, tight lipped during other passages.

'And this Lawrence, the Chief Constable, does he want you to let him know what is happening?'

'No. Definitely not. He told me that even you have instructions not to report back until what-ever-it-is is over.'

Jean nodded and looked relieved. 'I'm glad he made that plain. And if I may emphasise it. Lives are at stake. I cannot over stress the importance of the task we are engaged on.' She looked fiercely at Lance. 'So I must warn you if you do or say anything which might upset this - project, you will have to be silenced - understood.'

CHAPTER FIVE

The conversation at table had not been scintillating. Kirsty had spoken at length about her train ride up through the mountains to Zonza but seemed too tired to put much zest into her words. It was reputed to be one of the most beautiful and thrilling short train journeys in the world but Kirsty's repetitive outpourings of enthusiasm soon became boring and Albert Brodie's persistent questions on detail had not helped. The unaccustomed heat and the day's activity had induced a deep torpor; only the younger ones seemed to shake off this feeling as the day wore on.

This, and the freely available wine had made for a soporific evening but Lance could not sleep. Jean Two's parting comment when they had talked earlier kept coming back to his mind him like an ill digested meal. 'Silenced!' He rose soon after the first shafts of sunshine lit up the colourful curtains. He was at the pool before the sun had separated itself from the horizon. The water was cooler than in mid day so he swam a few vigorous lengths then, puffed by the unusual exertion, turned on his back and swam slowly but gracefully on the calm water.

A large, tough looking man, with a face as craggy as the surrounding hills and like them with lower slopes covered in scrubby growth, came out of the office block, looked around, then strode off. Lance heard a motor bike start off far down the road.

He looks a bit surreptitious, thought Lance, then, laughing at himself, dismissed it from his mind. The next person to appear was Jean. She was coming in the direction of the pool and Lance's expression was alternating uncertainly between the conspiratorial and the blank when she noticed him, switched on a quick smile, and hurried past.

Then Kirsty loomed over him at the poolside for a moment, slid silently into the water and swum in a business-like manner up and down the pool. She was dressed in a neat, black, one piece costume. As she climbed out of the pool water dripped from her rounded posterior. Lance decided she looked better without her drab clothes. She smiled at him but when he rose from the water she averted her eyes and darted off with a polite comment about seeing him at breakfast. Now alone by the pool Lance looked around and noted again how lovely the gardens were.

They were informal to the point of seeming neglect but the great variety of bushes appeared to have been expertly colour coordinated, the paths seemed higglety-pigglety but they were neatly kept and there were no notices forbidding anything or signs to mar the pleasant natural look. Daft to chase for drama when we can enjoy ourselves here without that, he thought, in fact this is what we really need. But he couldn't keep out of his mind that if anything nasty had happened to the elegant red head it must have happened very near to where he was now walking and within a three hour period of their arrival. He shuddered.

He took a round about series of tracks back to the villa persuading himself that he was enjoying the beauty of the garden but his eyes, alerted by the previous day's revelations, flicked around at every little movement. The birds picking at the recently watered ground rose in unison as a sixteen stone jogger in a yellow track suit plodded past with a grim self righteous look set on his face. Round the corner, shaking his head in disbelief at this apparition, came the Frenchman they had noticed at the wayside cafe. He was dressed like Noel Coward on a quiet day.

'Bonjour monsieur. Pourquois les Anglais toujours le jogajog.?'

'Je ne sais pas.' ventured Lance. Then thinking he would be better continuing in English. 'I think it is an American craze. They lead, we follow. You know - coke, hamburgers and psychiatrists. In France you have more sense.'

'Peut-etre - but not always. We now have a McDonalds in Paris,' he shrugged his shoulders in a gesture of despair, 'but than jogajog we have more interesting things to do.'

'You've got to keep fit to enjoy yourselves.'

'Nonsense one must conserve energy to enjoy oneself.'

'Maybe you're right. Talking of enjoying oneself. Have you seen the lovely green eyed red head we saw at the café – en route? I thought she was going to be with us. I had arranged to play tennis with her. I saw you talk to her.'

The Frenchman hesitated and looked as if he was trying to recall which woman Lance was referring to. 'There are many lovely women here. But perhaps I know the one you mean. I saw she had a tennis racket with her. You English. No, I have not seen her about since.'

'She must have gone somewhere else. Pity.'

'Chasing a man sans doubt.'

'Or avoiding one,' quipped Lance teasingly.

The Frenchman frowned then laughed appreciatively, patted Lance's shoulder and walked on and Lance looked after him. His well fitting suit covered a lean, slightly bony body. In spite of his casual manner he looked hard and fit. Lance rubbed his shoulder where the Frenchman had given him the friendly pat. It stung.

When Lance returned to the chalet there was a note from Caroline saying she had gone to breakfast. He dressed slowly and strolled to join her. She was already in earnest conversation with Ross who was telling her of the harbour attractions. There were evidently many boat tours on offer, mostly to beauty spots, fishing areas and beaches nearby but some going as far as Sardinia. He also mentioned a clay pigeon shooting club which met on Sundays in the village and shot over the sea along the coast from the harbour.

Lance asked Donna to recommend an interesting restaurant for lunch as they had decided to hire a car the next day to explore some of the countryside. She mentioned several but was particularly enthusiastic about an old restaurant in Sartene, an ancient town set high in the hills behind them.

'Go early and have a walk around first. It's full of beautiful lanes and alleys and hidden yards. It would be creepy in the dark but it's glorious on a day like this. There's plenty of shade when you get too hot and lots of little cafes. You'll love it.'

With some apprehension they phoned Lawrence as instructed. He was even more grave this time. 'A package from Judy has been received. That was quick. Must have used police channels. It contained a bloodstained handkerchief. They have applied DNA tests and it is from Jean Faulds' body. So, foul play. Your shot, perhaps. They didn't expect anything like this and contacted a young staff member who was on standby in the area to step in. She evidently speaks good French, is tough and doesn't look like a policewoman. I won't tell you what I think of that. It's all very sad. However not one moment of police time is to be wasted on that until the main task has been completed. So, unless she specifically asks for your help, which I am sure she won't, forget it and have a good holiday. Even the back up lass who I hear is a smart operator, is not allowed to report back.

Anyway, look after yourselves and have a great time. Bring Caroline round to dinner when you get home.'

They walked straight to the wine bar and found they were the first customers of the day.

'I don't understand the DNA bit. How can that work if they don't have the body to compare it with? Surely they don't keep DNA records of all police officers.' Lance sipped at his coffee without tasting it.

'I don't know. But they could get some blood from a relative – a parent or sister. That would tell them near enough certainly, I would think. Imagine having to go and ask for a sample and having to explain why you wanted it. Who would be a policeman?'

'Yes. That must have been a rotten job. I'll bet they sent a policewoman.'

'But I still didn't like it when he said they weren't going to waste a moment looking for poor Jean.'

'Exactly what I was thinking. When I tell Lawrence what I think of that next time we see him it will curdle his claret.'

Caroline rose leaving her coffee untouched. 'Let's go for a walk.'

They strode up the hills at a cracking pace without talking. They sat down and gazed at the sea without seeing it; smelled the maquis without savouring it. After a time they walked down the hill holding hands; something they did not often do.

Now tiring they strolled slowly round that part of the village beyond the harbour. Here they also found cafes in every corner, some brash and modern, many ice cream parlours but also a few typical Corsican coffee rooms. They chose one of the latter. Lance enjoyed a handsome example of the local patisserie.

Afterwards as they walked along the coast towards the harbour a repeated but irregular cracking noise disturbed the quiet.

'Guns,' said Lance. 'That'll be the clay pigeon set up. Let's have a look.'

'Pity we have to have that noise in a place like this - and on a Sunday,' complained Caroline.

'Only day the locals have time to have a go I expect.'

'Well, better than shooting real birds. I wonder if young Ross has come down to have a go. He sounded interested.'

They sauntered, it was already hot, along the rough shoreline away from the main promenade. Here they could look up at the untidy backs of the buildings whose meticulously tidy fronts lined the main street. Balconies, which seemed to have only tenuous connections with the buildings, clung on with a mixture of bright flowers and colourful washing dangling from them. There were not many people about but as the sounds of gunfire grew louder they saw a group clustered together further along the shore. As they drew near they saw that clay pigeons were hurtling into the air from a small trench on the untidy beach. The bright orange targets were going off in a variety of directions so that the man at the gun had to aim left then right, low as one skimmed the surface of the sea then high as one disappeared towards the white sun. The local who was shooting was scoring about two thirds of the time. No voices were heard raised in appreciation or otherwise by the solemn watchers - only the marksman's curse every time a clay was missed.

'Maybe if the creator had made birds which shattered into little bits like that men wouldn't shoot them,' suggested Caroline.

'The creator made foxes inedible,' countered Lance.

The local shot broke his gun and went off and the man in the pit nodded invitingly to a young man in the small crowd. He stepped forward and they saw that it was Ross looking younger than ever among the sun dried faces around him. A brown faced man handed him a gun. He appeared nervous and protested a lack of experience which became obvious as soon as he started. After some wild misses the trapper catapulted some easier ones for him and in the end he was scoring the occasional hit with the satisfying scatter of the clay fragments across the sky. When he had fired his last shot and turned away with a half smile on his face a large man pushed forward, a nicely polished gun in his hands, and set about demolishing everything that was put in the air with almost contemptuous ease. His final flourish was the disintegrating of a small fish which had foolishly flipped out of the water. As he shouldered his way though the crowd Lance recognised him as the large man who had come out of the office when he was swimming. He was dressed as then in a checked shirt and dark trousers held up by a broad belt. He looked just like Desperate Dan - a favourite of Lance's comic reading days. The trapper looked around. Lance stepped forward escaping the clutching hands of Caroline who desperately wanted a low profile day.

Not knowing if the French for pull was the correct instruction Lance made a loud grunt that sounded like the big man's command. Lance missed the first two clays and Caroline crept over towards Ross not to be associated with the embarrassment. Lance then flung the gun up and down in his hands and braced himself. The next clay leapt out straight in front of him and burst into fragments. The trapper started to vary the shots yet each clay shattered in front of their eyes. Caroline watched goggle eyed. With one shot to go the pigeon was sent off just inches above the water and Lance managed to wing it. The trapper nodded.

'You have hidden talents,' said Caroline gripping his arm possessively, 'Where did you learn that?'

'Some things come naturally to a man.'

'Rubbish. There's only one thing comes naturally to a man. You've done that before.'

'A sniping course at Achnacarry with the Lovat scouts. They scoffed at shooting static targets. We did this for fun. I was quite good.'

'You were marvellous. You can ride shotgun for me any time. So your national service was not just to get shot of your virginity.'

'I can assure you I more success with guns than with girls; easier to understand.' He paused. 'Did you know that the bloke who shot before me comes up to the Villas? I've seen him slip out of the office looking very sheepish for a big lad like him.'

'I have heard that one of the sisters has a large friend. Might be him.'

'That was a display.'

'You mean like a mating display?'

'No. Quite the reverse. A keep off display. A little warning.'

'To whom?' She paused. 'Not to us I hope.'

'Perhaps including us. He looked around as if asserting his dominance like a stag.'

'That's mating.'

'You're getting to have a one track mind woman. Keep working at it. No, this was a macho display. Did you notice that you were the only woman there? This was a - I am not just a big rough neck - demonstration.'

'He won't have liked your brilliant efforts then.'

'That did occur to me.'

CHAPTER SIX

At dinner that night Ross talked of the shooting and praised, somewhat enviously, Lance's display of marksmanship. He also told them how he had been involved in a conversation with Raoul, as the large local was called, and after introducing himself but not giving much information about himself the big man had asked him to meet him next day if he was interested in doing a little job for him.

'He said he wanted a young athletic type so I said I'd go and hear what he had in mind.' He turned to Ian. 'You can come along if you like.'

'I like to know what I'm letting myself in for.'

'Well, I never turn down the chance to make some money. I've got big ideas for the future but I need some money to get started. Come and see what he says. Commits you to nothing.'

'Right,' agreed Ian, 'but I'm not wasting sunshine or opportunities for a few bob. I'm here for the high life.'

'Do you know him, Donna?' asked Lance. 'Comes about here. I've seen him go into the office. An ugly brute. Weighs about half a ton.'

'No, but I know who you mean. Rhoda seems to like him but Mona doesn't have much time for him.'

'That sounds like sisters.' Caroline snorted.

Donna nodded. 'I go to Rhoda if I have to speak to either of them. She's easier. Mona blew my head off about breakages and a measly one sheet short in the count - but I don't see much of either of them. You don't if you do your job.'

'Well, no harm in finding out what he's after. And if there is any harm going to be done I think I'd like to be on Roaul's side.' Ross rose from the table and took some dishes into the kitchen and was rewarded with a smile from Donna. She raised her voice and spoke from there.

'He must be very strong. Last week two pall bearers stumbled going up the hill to the graveyard with a coffin and the big fella took one end of the box by himself - and it's a fair climb.'

Caroline gave an involuntary nod in agreement.

'Coffins can be heavy,' said Lance. Caroline now gave an involuntary shudder.

'Could there have been two bodies in the coffin?' asked Caroline when they were back in their room.'

'Go to sleep.' said Lance.

But Lance himself could not sleep. He tossed noisily to Caroline's strongly expressed displeasure then just when the worries of the day were fading a dreadful roaring shattered the normal tranquillity of the evenings at Villamaquis.

'The local yobs out on their bikes. It'll pass soon. I hope they're going on a long journey.'

But they were not. They circled round and round. Each time when it seemed as if it were coming to an end up it started again. It was almost half an hour before the couple could settle themselves for slumber again. But Lance still could not sleep. The thought of the body of the lovely red head pressed into a coffin with the remains of the deceased Fournier haunted and disgusted him. Then when he had made up his mind what he was going to do he lay quite still till the first lightening of the sky.

Lance dressed quietly in both senses. He made it out of the room without disturbing his now peacefully sleeping wife and in his most sober attire stalked self consciously towards the gate. He heard gentle splashing from the direction of the pool and turning his head he could just discern two naked swimmers slowly traversing the pool and whispering. He paused then, with a pang of envy, turned his mind to the gruesome task ahead.

He had no difficulty finding the exotic graveyard but as he stumbled through the undergrowth and long dank grass he wished he had paid more attention to Caroline's description of her route to the grave. He had briefly thought of waking her to ask for details but dismissed that thought as soon as it came to him. She would not have been best pleased either by the disturbance or the destination. He now found he was constantly climbing, sometimes up steep paths, occasionally up stone steps. It occurred to him that the little buildings seem to be arranged in a way which gave each occupant the best possible view over the bay. Some of the crypts had colourful arrangements of flowers at the front but they seemed superfluous as wild flowers grew on every patch of soil and from every crack in the steps and paving stones. The fresh cut flowers bravely competed with nature's exhibition but the week old drooping displays were made to look pathetic amidst the constantly renewing display of poppies, white heather, lavender and tiny buttercups.

He passed a gloomy structure which looked like a stone filing cabinet. Three of the four sections were blocked by neat marble slabs but the fourth was open, empty and waiting. He was now seeing things not mentioned by Caroline and feared he had lost the way. In fact having entered the wooded area by that gate he had little choice and after only two wrong turnings was soon standing by the fallen angel.

He gave it a friendly pat then looked round for the crow. It did not appear. He advanced slowly examining each crypt closely. Some he dismissed because the family name, not Fournier, was clearly displayed. Some he passed by because they had obviously not been disturbed for years. As soon as his eye fell on the right one he knew this was it. The door looked scarred and the marks on the ground could have been made that morning. He shivered.

He laid his plastic bag on the ground and took out a large screw driver - it had been the nearest thing to a jemmy he had been able to find in the chalet. He pushed it hard into the gap between the door and the stone surround. It yielded almost too quickly for him and the door was not too difficult to pull open enough for him to squeeze through. None of the insurmountable difficulties he had been subconsciously hoping for came to his rescue and he found himself inside the crypt.

He carefully put the screw driver back into the bag and took out a torch. He shivered at the thought of Caroline in here without a light and she moved up a notch in his estimation. The coffin lay there and Lance looked at it hypnotised for a long time. He then stepped forward and looked more closely. He had no idea how a coffin lid was secured. To his relief he saw screw heads. He examined the screwdrivers in his bag and tried a smaller one. It was an approximate fit. The screws were not as tight as he had feared but he was no do-it-yourself man and he had to pause at least twice during the turning of each screw. The muscles in the palms of his hands and up his forearms were aching. Sweat ran stickily and made his grip even less strong. It took him a long time to release the last of the screws. He carefully laid it in the row on the floor where he had placed the other screws in the order they would have to be replaced just as if he were changing a car wheel.

He stood back and leaned against the wall and braced himself for the next step. Tears were running down his cheeks. He dabbed his nose with Caroline's profusely perfumed handkerchief and levered open the coffin lid. He reached for the torch and shone it into the coffin.

He was about to lower his eyes which he had very deliberately kept pointing upwards when he heard faint footsteps outside. Someone was coming slowly and cautiously towards the crypt.

Lance lowered the lid and darted to the crevice by the door and peered out. He had a very restricted arc of view and could see nothing but the dark, ominous trees but he could still hear the slow careful steps coming closer. He looked around in panic for a place to hide. His eyes lit on the coffin shining where the shaft of light struck its mahogany surface. He shook his head in horror at the idea of hiding in it, bent down and picked up the biggest screw driver. It now seemed very small and light. But even in his intense state of panic Lance worked out that whoever was out there shouldn't be there or he would be moving more freely so he braced himself for action feeling very like the proverbial cornered rat somewhat comforted by the thought that the person who corners the rat doesn't feel too good either. The footsteps ceased for some time then more, a little closer, a pause, then closer still. Lance could now see a shadow. It was only about ten feet away. Lance twisted his head round so that he would get an early sight of anyone coming in that direction. The next moment the shadow was replaced by substance. He instantly recognised whose substance.

Lance waited until the step was right by the door then let out a piercing shriek and yelled 'Mon Dieu! Mon Dieu! Allez! Allez vous en! Souffrez que je dorme tranquille.' followed by a mixture of all the strong sounding French words he could think of all the time banging hard on the door. Then he emitted another long moaning scream. He now saw Albert Brodie scrambling pell mell down the hill, stumbling and falling, rising and running as if something dreadful was right by his shoulder. Lance thought of Tam o Shanter. The tall thin man passed out of the field of view doing an inelegant somersault.

Lance now turned back to his task, fearful that he might have alarmed someone other than the hapless Brodie, knowing that if so he could procrastinate no longer. He shone the torch towards the coffin and hesitated only for a moment before lifting the lid. He examined the contents of the coffin with great care, turned away, spoke out loud to himself what he had seen then turned back and rechecked. Like Kim's game at the Scouts, he laughed grimly to himself. He picked up a small hard fragment which glittered in the folds of satin at the bottom of the coffin avoiding as much as possible contact with the cold body in the pristine white winding sheet then picked up the four tiny fragments which met his fingers and twisted them up in his own handkerchief. As quickly as his shaking hands allowed he screwed the lid back on. He fumbled with one screw and lost it between the slabs on the floor. Before he left he flashed the light around looking for bloodstains. To his intense relief the floor was spotless. On second thoughts this alarmed him even more and like Caroline before him he found himself bowing and mumbling an apology to the now oft disturbed corpse.

Caroline had just finished showering when he entered the chalet. As he came towards her she swerved to avoid the usual affectionate fondle. To her surprise he pushed past without a glance at her glistening body. He dropped his clothes in an untidy heap on the floor and stepped into the still pouring shower.

'A drink,' he growled

Caroline's eyebrows shot up.

'Please.'

Caroline sensing the urgency in his voice, pulled on her shower robe, broached the duty free and handed him a glass of neat brandy. It became diluted as he stood under the cascade sipping the burning fluid. He kept sipping long after it had become neat water.

'Give me that.' Caroline grabbed the glass and refilled it. He declined the glass and started soaping himself feverishly.

'What have you been up to? What is that smell? Perfume. Lance what have you been up to? Lance speak to me. Listen if you've been caught up in the Hedonism of this place tell me about it. I might understand.' She took a sip at the brandy. She spluttered.

'Too early for me. And too early for you. No wonder you feel bad if there's been hanky panky at this time of the morning. If some young girl has taken advantage of you she might have waited until the engine was warm and the choke was back in. What a mess these clothes are in. I'll never get these stains out. I'll bung them all in the laundry basket. Ah! No need to scrub away to get rid of the perfume. It's here.' She paused in her furious rant and held up the handkerchief which Lance had soaked in her favourite perfume and put it to her nose. 'She must be a right tart to wear a perfume like this. Lance I thought you had taste.'

Lance slumped into a wicker chair still naked and wet. He had heard little of the outburst. He saw the handkerchief and started to apologise for taking it.

'Sorry darling I -'

'Don't sorry me. I want an explanation before I'm ready for any sorrys. A real man would have sneaked in quietly and that would have been that. And hide that - that body.' She threw a towel at him and left the room.

'Hide that body.' Lance's head fell on his hands and he started to tremble. He could just hear Caroline's voice raised in the background but he did not hear any words. She continued to rant on mainly to stop herself thinking. She didn't want to think. Getting no response she glanced in and saw the shaking figure.

'Here it's me who should be upset. Unless you were raped or something. A big man like you. Look, let me rub you. And stop that. Pull yourself together.' She rubbed his back for a short time then, thoroughly confused and getting angry she threw the towel at him and growled. 'I'm going to dress and have breakfast. You come if you like.'

It was a strange breakfast. Both Lance and Albert were absent as was Ross. But the latter's place was taken by a pretty pert young lady. Ian introduced her in a matter of fact way as a friend and they certainly behaved in a friendly manner to each other. Ross had evidently declared his intention to be elsewhere that night and Ian had taken advantage of the vacant bed - and probably the girl. To Caroline she seemed a pleasant lass but she was not in the mood to be sociable in the circumstances. Ian was obviously disappointed - he liked Caroline and regarded her as a free thinker which indeed she had been until half an hour previously.

'Lance still in bed. Had a hard night' he mocked cheerfully.

'Mind your own business,' she snapped. Ian turned to Mabel but the flat look silenced him before he got started so he gave his undivided attention to his companion of the night. Jean expressed serious concern for Lance and Caroline found that even more difficult. Kirsty babbled on about a stream she had found with little recessed caves under each waterfall. Jean warned her to stay clear of them as they were extremely dangerous. She recommended another stream which opened out into small pools deep enough to swim in with white smooth rocks to sun bathe on. Before they split up Donna asked if they would all be on time for dinner as she and Meryl were putting on their famed, they described it thus, Corsican souffle. Keep it secret she warned or the Corsican Sisters will be up and they will gobble the lot. Caroline rose from the table she had had enough of secrets for one day.

Lance was dressed and had recovered his composure when Caroline re-entered the chalet. He had a determined look on his face but when he saw the expression on Caroline's face he couldn't help laughing. 'If you think I've been out screwing all night you're not far wrong.'

Caroline sat down heavily on the bed and dipped her eyes.

Lance let her sit there quietly for a moment then continued very softly. 'Screwing off a coffin lid.' He held up two claw-like, cramped, cut hands. 'Look.'

She lifted her eyes and slowly the significance of his remark sunk in. 'You didn't? You haven't?'

'And I'd better return this tart's handkerchief.' He handed the fragment of cotton to her.

She let it drop on the floor. 'Why? What's the point now?'

'I had to see if she was there. In the box. Yuck!'

'And was she?'

'No, but Monsieur Fournier didn't look as tidy as I thought he would be in the circumstances.'

'They let him fall, remember.'

'Yes, but it was more than that. Maybe not. But I had the feeling - I don't know - I can't express how I felt. How tightly do they screw down coffin lids?'

'How would I know? Fairly tight I would think. They would have power screwdrivers probably. Why?'

'It was tough getting the screws out but not as tough as I had feared. I would have had more of a struggle taking down a baby's cot.'

'If I remember right you didn't manage that. I had to do it.'

'I wasn't well that day. Anyway I would happily have let you do it this morning.'

He uncurled his cramped hands. Lance had taken to the furniture trade because of his admiration for anyone who could saw straight, never mind the super men who could contrive a mitre, engineer a dovetail or use a screwdriver effortlessly. His genuine appreciation of the craftsmen had made him the ideal person to run a furniture store and workshop as his appreciation in turn gained the respect of his workers.

He frowned when the vision of the crypt came back to him. 'Look, let's pick up the car. I've got one or two things to tell you where we can't be overheard.'

They asked for a small vehicle and were allocated a red Volkswagen Polo. They drove up a quiet road and stopped in a large maquis covered area overlooking the sea. Brilliantly coloured small bushes spread up the slopes behind them as far as the eye could see like a painting by a mad, exuberant impressionist. A strong perfume filled the car. They sat quietly for a long time watching the tiny yachts in the distance and the even smaller windsurfers. Lance fancied he saw Ross skim up to a raft moored off shore and talk to someone sunbathing on it. Then he noticed a rowing boat low in the water but moving at a fair speed.

'That looks like our friend Raoul. An all rounder. Somehow he looks out of place on the water but he can certainly make that boat shift. Who is that with him?'

'I'm not even sure it is Raoul. But it is certainly someone with muscles. I think his passenger is sea sick. Her face is over the water. I can't make out who it is.' Caroline stopped talking, leant back in her seat and waited for Lance's revelations.

'Brodie was there.' Lance broke the silence. He then, slowly and in detail, explained the intrusion and how he had frightened off the prowler.

'If you had done that to me I would have dropped dead.'

'Where better?'

'We'd better tell Jean about this.' suggested Caroline.

'Yes. I've been trying to think how. I don't want her to know we've been interfering. Lawrence wouldn't be happy to hear that. And I want to stay on her right side in the hope she'll tell us a bit more about what's going on.'

'Why not just say you saw Brodie going into the graveyard? It would be true. You could say you were out jogging. No. Walking might be more credible. Couldn't sleep. Which would also be true. She knows neither of you were down for breakfast.'

'Yes, I'll do that. Someone will have to keep on eye on that man. I'm surprised she wasn't having him followed after our warning.'

'We don't know if she has assistance. And she has to sleep. I do hope she's not on her own. We should repeat our offer to help. As long as it doesn't involve any more graveyards.' Caroline paused and pursed her lips. 'This must be a big deal if the loss of a young lass can be written off by the powers that be. That's obviously what Jean Two thinks. It makes me wonder about her. I just don't believe in that attitude. We little people matter too.'

She shook her head. 'What else did you find out? Was Fournier a big man?'

'About average. In fact I thought coffins if not made to measure were selected for a reasonably good fit. This one had plenty of room.'

'For what?'

'Don't. I can't bear to think about it. I went out there this morning to get shot of these fears. I'm not sure we're any further forward. Oh, and there wasn't any blood on the floor. Not even a dried up stain.'

'Well, there was when I was there I can assure you. It wouldn't be raspberry juice. Not there. It was a shiny floor - marble maybe. It would be easy to wipe it up.'

'But who? Not Brodie. Unless he goes there every morning to tidy up.'

'I don't think so. Or why would he be back again so soon. No somebody else is doing something and Brodie doesn't know about it. This gets complicated. I wonder if Jean herself has been up. After what you said she might have wanted to check it herself. Maybe she does care and has had the girl's body taken away for a decent burial.'

'I hope so. I hate the thought of her spending all eternity with a man she had never met. Not right. You know I'd like to get the man who did this. I'd break his bloody ,'-- Lance gritted his teeth.

'Well, let's tell Jean first. But no hint that we're messing about in her patch. Then we'll hear what she says and make up our mind what we can do - if anything.'

'And let's not think too badly of Jean Two. Remember she is a police officer – and she must know she might be the next little cog to be written off.' Caroline nodded and Lance continued. 'Oh! I almost forgot. I rummaged about in the bottom of the coffin.' He grued at the recollection. 'And I picked up these.' He showed her a small shiny fragment. 'What can that be?'

Caroline took the piece reluctantly and held it away from herself. She examined it carefully for some time.

'Plastic. I can't think what but it looks faintly familiar. Of course it might be his – Fournier's - or the undertaker's - or from one of the many intruders.' She thrust it back into his hands as if it were too hot.

'Or it might be hers.'

Lance nodded and handed her the next items.

'Two seeds? Maybe grape seeds.'

And of the next she ventured. 'A wood shaving.'

Lance took back the curl of wood. 'Yes. Oak. I would have thought it would have been veneered chipboard. Unless he was very well to do. A roadman the obit said. A very high quality coffin for a roadman. Worth a thought.' He paused in recollection.

'And there were dark marks inside the coffin - on the fabric – the lining. But the shroud was squeaky clean.'

'What kind of marks?'

'Well, they weren't footprints.'

'Lance!'

'Sorry. I don't like this conversation. They were stains. Might have been blood.'

'At the top or in the middle?'

Lance looked puzzled. 'Why not the bottom?'

'Because it is unusual to kill someone by slitting their ankles or bashing their feet with a blunt implement.'

'Right, smarty. The stains were at the bottom.'

Caroline scratched her head then, 'Of course top and tail. That would be where the head of a second corpse would be.'

Lance shook his head in distaste, shut his eyes and whispered. 'If you say so.'

They drove down to the chalets but Jean had gone - no-one knew where so they decided to have a rest and catch Jean at souffle time.

Jean, like all the others, even Ross, appeared at the table sharp on time. The souffle was a triumph, a culinary masterpiece and drove all thoughts of graves and bloodstains from their mind. It was made in one large dish and had risen as high as it was broad. The thin, crisp crust was various shades of gold. It was light yet didn't just disappear on the plate when served. There was a flavour of cheese but also subtle suggestions of the sea in it. Donna and Meryl had put on little white chef's hats and looked very pretty. The souffle and favourite foods, recipes and restaurants, were the topics of conversation for the entire meal which suited Lance and Caroline perfectly.

Jean was reluctant to return with them to their chalet so the trio met by the tennis court. They sat at a table set in the trees to give shade in mid day. The sun was not quite set and two couples were still playing on the courts. The floodlighting cast crisscrossing shadows. Anyone passing invariably looked towards the courts so the meeting was as private as they could have wished; even the laughter from the players seemed to give an aural smokescreen to the earnest discussion.

As agreed they told Jean only that Lance had witnessed Albert's visit to the graveyard.

Jean exploded. 'What the hell is he up to?' She then cross examined Lance in a way which implied, to start with, that she didn't believe him. Luckily Lance by telling the truth, if not the whole truth, was able to convince her. She sat there shaking her head in bewilderment. She seemed to be turning over in her mind alternative courses of action none of which really appealed to her.

The request she now made had the tone of an order. 'Look I have to follow another trail. Could you keep an eye on this man for me - just for the next two days? I'll clear it with the Chief Constable if there's any fuss. I have vital matters to attend to today and tomorrow. I can't spare a minute and this man might just spoil everything.'

Caroline shook her head in disbelief. 'He doesn't look like a very dangerous man.'

'Which, if he is involved, is exactly why he is just the sort of man who would be chosen for this sort of thing. Was I right in thinking you were willing to help?'

Lance looked at his wife who gave him the slightest nod. 'Right, we'll do what we can. But I haven't followed anyone since I left High School - and even then she usually guessed what I was after.' Jean showed no appreciation of the humour. 'I mean we can't stalk him. He'd rumble us in minutes.'

'I'm sure that's true - but just find out what he is doing, be near him as much as you can, even befriend him if need be and give me a note of how he spends the days. Just where he goes and if possible who he speaks to. But whatever he does don't tackle him, accuse him or tell him what you are up to.'

'Or we'll be silenced.' said Lance jocularly.

'Exactly.' replied Jean seriously.

As they rose to go Lance asked. 'Do you think Jean Faulds was up there?'

'No. I am Jean Faulds.' Again this sounded like an order.

They lay in bed saying not a word. Caroline was the first to break the spell. 'Have you been silenced already?'

'I'm thinking. There's something not right about Albert Brodie as a big baddie. I think he is just a wee cog. Maybe a decoy. Unless he is a superb actor he just doesn't have the gravitas for a big part in this sort of thing. Let's do what Jean asked but let's keep looking around. I think she underestimates our talents.'

'So do I.' mumbled Caroline as she turned and composed herself for sleep.

CHAPTER SEVEN

Caroline woke first and was tiptoeing out of the room when Lance spoke sharply. 'Where the hell are you going?'

'For a breath of air, darling.'

'You're not going up to that accursed graveyard are you? Promise me you're not going there.'

'If you open you're dozy eyes and cast them on your gorgeous wife you will see she is in a flimsy dressing gown. I promise you I only visit grave yards fully clothed. I'm not into black masses - anyway they take place in the dark don't they?'

'Where are you off to then?'

'I'm not off anywhere. I am going to sit on the verandah, breath in the lovely air and look. I'd like to get a sense of the tempo of this place. Get the background. Some of it must relate to what's happening in the foreground.'

The air was already quite warm but the plastic of the patio bench was cold through her thin garments. She stood up and leaned on the upright. She was partly obscured by cascades of bougainvillaea. The air was heavy with perfume and not a breath of wind stirred it. As she looked round she appreciated how cleverly the grounds had been laid out. She could see no other building and of the paths she could observe only short stretches, with no real idea where any passersby had come from or where they were going.

For a long time she saw no-one. The first couple were in swim suits so she had no difficulty with them. She then saw Ross heading uphill so guessed he was returning to his chalet. It crossed her mind to hope that his bed was not occupied. The phut phut of a low powered motor cycle now reached her ears and she noted the time. She also noted that he seemed to stop some way off. The next figure to come into view some time later was, she was sure, that of the bus driver who had brought them from the air port. He passed between two bright bushes and disappeared roughly in the direction of the offices. Just before Lance joined her she saw Jean walk briskly downhill.

'What's all this then?' asked Lance as he slipped his arms round her waist.

'It's lovely. Better than graveyards. It really is a most gorgeous place. Some people are enjoying it.'

'I was. I needed that sleep. Well - learn anything?'

'I'm not sure. I'm going to write down the comings and goings. See if we can establish any pattern. Someone around here knows what happened to the real Jean. Rest her soul.'

Lance was so engrossed watching two long legged young girls scampering about the tennis courts that Caroline eventually went herself for the cooling drink she had been suggesting for some time. She came back with two cold drinks and a hot flustered face.

'Sorry dear. I meant to -.'

'Never mind that.' She leant close to Lance's ear although the chance of anyone overhearing above the screams of delight from the courts was slight. 'I had to sign for these drinks.' She paused for effect.

One of the young girls with a very short skirt leapt high for a ball and minimized the effect.

'Listen, you randy old man. This is important.'

He was about to protest as he always did about the epithet old when he noticed the serious look on her face. 'Yes. I'm all ears.'

'That'll be a change. As I was saying, before the knickers interrupted me, I had to sign the book. I saw that Jean signed it on the day we arrived.' She paused. This time she had his full attention. 'The signature is by the same hand as wrote the label you risked so much to get. So she must have gone for a drink almost as soon as we arrived.'

'Well, well. Well done. It was certainly hot. I remember the same thought occurred to me but I didn't know about the signing bit and couldn't face the hassle of the money until we got sorted out. So we now know one of her moves between arriving and --,' his voice tailed off.

'So - usual question. Do we tell Jean?'

'If she's any good she'll have noticed that herself. She'll get fed up with us if we run with every detail. Let's sit on this and see if we can find out if anyone saw her. She was fairly conspicuous. So full of life.'

'Don't.'

Lance could not bring himself to continue watching the girls on the court just because they were still, so abundantly, full of life.

'Let's go have a word with Donna. She was on duty that day. She might have seen her. And if she didn't that tells us something too.'

'You ask her. Your interest in the movements of the red head would be more credible than mine. But not a word that Jean Two has taken her place. I have a feeling that that being known would not be helpful to our police lady.'

Lance, dressed in whites, walked up to Donna with his tennis racket in his hand. 'Ah Donna. Have you seen any sign of the red head who arrived on the first day?' Donna looked at him with a - aren't you married - look on her face. 'We arranged to play tennis,' he continued, 'But she hasn't turned up. I'm sure it was for today. I haven't seen her about since the day we arrived to confirm the arrangement.'

Donna was emphatic that she had not seen anyone of that description and was not aware of any changes arranged among the occupants of her group of chalets. Lance didn't press the matter further as he could think of no way of doing so without saying too much. He asked Donna if she could join him to add verisimilitude to his tale. She regretted - she was too busy.

When he reported to Caroline she summed up the knowledge they now had of that fateful three hours between arrival and assembling for the first meal together.

'We arrived around four. She almost certainly took her luggage to her chalet. Agreed?'

'Agreed.'

'At some time in the next say two and three quarter hours she went down to the bar, helped herself to a drink and signed the book.'

'And that's all we know.'

'Not quite. We can also think backwards. Jean two must have learned somehow that her colleague had been - waylaid and we assume phoned for instructions. She also found the blood stained handkerchief and despatched that back to the police in Britain which, almost certainly, meant a visit to the village unless she has help here. After that she went to the chalet, changed, she wasn't exactly trendy but she was freshly dressed, and come then to the table. That all took time. She was the last to arrive but she was only ten minutes late at the most. It's hard to imagine that the waylaying - or whatever - took place less than half an hour before then. So we have lost about twenty minutes off the front end and at least forty minutes off the back end. Therefore whatever happened to her happened between about four twenty and six.'

'At a time when most people were sorting themselves out after the journey. Then showering and getting ready for dinner.'

'The shot,' groaned Caroline. 'That was the time of your shot — you know the shot that didn't travel far.'

'You're right. So we can be specific. If that was a shot. And we now have to face the possibility that it could well have been. It must have been just after we unpacked and tucked away our things. So she must have gone down for her drink just as soon as she arrived. Oh, why didn't I report that shot?'

'Because no one would have paid a blind bit of notice to you. You told Lawrence and he didn't seem to put much weight on it. It was, most likely, just a coincidence.'

Lance ignored that last remark. 'I am trying to remember how the shot sounded. Muffled it was. If it was the sound of a gun I think she was shot at very close quarters and – probably indoors.'

'In her chalet, perhaps.'

'Almost certainly.' He shuddered. 'Did you look to see if any one else had signed the book at the same time?

'That same thought had just occurred to me. No, I did not. I was too excited. You don't have to put a time in the book so we wouldn't learn exactly when whoever signed after her had been in the bar. But I agree it might still be useful know who it was. Let's go have a look to see which were the names closest to hers.'

'Right, another drink.'

They poured their juice on the ground when no one was looking and made for the bar. There on the counter was shining a new book.

Some time later Lance asked Caroline. 'Why did Jean One sign the book? Wine and soft drinks are on the house.'

'She can't have noticed that.'

'Some policewoman. What did she have to drink?'

'An orange juice I think. I was in such a hurry to get back to you I didn't look too carefully. I just saw that the writing was the same - sort of plain and authoritative. I thought we would look at it together when we went back." She paused and her eyebrows came together as she thought hard. Lance looked at her speculatively but said nothing.

'I'm trying to recall the entry in the book. You know I have a feeling that she signed for more than one drink. That same handwriting continued after the orange juice. I am sure it was orange juice. I didn't read on but I can see it in my mind's eye. I'd swear she wrote something else. Could she have been drinking with another person. Of course that person could have been Jean Two.'

'Well, knowing what whoever was with her was drinking might help us find out who it was. We must get a sight of that book.'

'If it hasn't been destroyed.'

'Then we'll have saved a few euros in drinking money.'

'Let's put together our notes on the movements of our friends and neighbours,' suggested Lance.

'Well, I've got Raoul coming every morning about six, by motor cycle and leaving about six forty five but I don't know who he comes here to see.'

'So, that's one to check.'

'I'd better do that. I wouldn't like you to be damaged by him. He's less likely to have a go at me.'

'I second that.'

'Our French friend walks about the grounds about seven - and it can't be for exercise - he moves too slowly.'

'Can't sleep.'

'Maybe.'

'The sisters go into the office also about seven thirty. They seem to come from that house high up on the hill. What a wonderful view they must have. Right over the bay. Donna or Meryl arrive at our kitchen at eight. All our group seem to come straight from bed to breakfast except Kirsty who always has a walk up the hill. That's it apart from the days when Albert and you go visiting graveyards.'

'The bus from the airport comes every second day. Jean has irregular movements but then she would have. She comes in very late some nights.'

'Yes, I worry for her. I do hope she knows what she is doing.'

'And Ross comes for breakfast every second morning. Ah the first correlation -'

'That's a good word.'

'Ross is not with us for breakfast on the same day as the bus goes to the airport.'

'Good. And Ian's movements have no pattern.'

'How about the Corsican sisters? Do they go out at all?'

'I haven't seen much of them. They never take the bus which is understandable. They both have small cars. Renaults. One is a convertible - I think that one's Rhoda's.'

'Ever seen anyone drive with them?'

'No, never. Not that I've seen much of them full stop. I believe the only time they join the guests is at the weekly grand barbeque buffet.'

'Right, let's be there then.'

'We can perhaps risk talking about the red head and see if anyone else noticed her.'

'Which some one must have unless a magician spirited her away. But no. I don't think in this close little community we can talk to anyone about her. We might well be talking to the killer.'

CHAPTER EIGHT

'I learned to stalk with the Lovat Scouts but even Scottish heather would be easier on the knees than these pavements and give bit more cover.' Lance joked as he saw with dismay the sloping uneven pavements of the ancient town.

'If you intend to go on your knees pretend you're doing a penance. This is a good Catholic country. No one would give you a second glance. Look stop messing about they're getting too far ahead.'

Talk of the barbeque had made our couple think of food and so when they heard the Brodies agreeing to go in the resort bus to Sartene, Lance and Caroline had driven up the steep road after them hoping to lunch at the restaurant recommended by Donna. They had gone past the bus and arrived ahead of them to avoid creating any suspicion that they were following and had, for this purpose, made themselves quite conspicuous in the Square when the bus arrived so that their presence would not be a shock. They even exchanged surprised hallos and compared favourable first impressions of the venerable buildings; high cliff like grey edifices, much taller and older than the tenements of the British industrial revolution.

Since then it had not been easy. They passed the most charming, attractive, tempting cafes both in the open squares and in the narrow twisting passages, and as the time wore nearer to midday equally alluring bars but the Brodies strode steadily onwards visiting every church, monument and graveyard. Albert took a great interest in the latter examining them carefully and jotting in a small notebook.

'Maybe he's looking for a place to move the body to. Do you think he is taking measurements. An old grave must be the ideal hiding place. He's realised a recently used one is far too busy.' Lance forced a laugh.

'Some of these haven't been disturbed for centuries. I'm keeping a note of the ones Bones Brodie is showing a special interest in. It should be easy to check if they've been disturbed.'

'You mean we spend our holiday keeping tombs under surveillance'

'We're only half an hour away. One of us could check each day. It's a lovely run.'

Just then the couple they were following disappeared into a modern plastic faced cafe. It could not have been further from the restaurant recommended by Donna, in ambience or, Lance guessed, gastronomically.

Lance looked around desperately. 'I'm not going in there. That's beyond the call of duty. Graveyards yes but juke boxes no.' He now noticed a quiet brown painted bar with an open courtyard in front furnished with wooden tables bleached lightest grey. 'Look. The ideal place to keep an eye on them from.'

They picked a shaded corner from which they could see the entrance to the cafe and ordered two beers one large and one small; a change from the free flowing free wine. They could see Mabel's back. She was sitting on a pavement table and was soon tucking into a large hamburger in a roll.

'Now they look at home.' Caroline ordered some local cheeses and crusty bread and she and Lance felt very non tourist.

'Did you know that this very town is where the word vendetta originated?' asked Caroline.

Lance looked across the road at the couple he was learning to hate and replied, 'No, I did not but I can now understand why.'

'The original one lasted for generations. Isn't it wonderful how bad ideas spread so efficiently throughout the world?'

They settled down to enjoy a leisurely munch when they saw the couple opposite call for their bill so, with great reluctance and much cursing, they bolted most of the remainder of their delicious lunch. Caroline set off after the Brodies while Lance settled the bill. This gave him the chance to have another two pulls at his beer which he left with a longing backward glance.

Within half an hour the Brodies were on the bus going back down the hill followed by the frustrated Lockharts.

The Brodies disappeared into their chalet as Lance turned the car into the Villamaquis and seemed to settle down for a siesta over the hottest part of the day. The Lockharts lay on recliners, half dozing in the sunshine, facing straight down the path to the Brodie chalet. Caroline squeezed herself into a corner of their balcony so that she could see a segment of that chalet.

Lance dropped off occasionally but not Caroline. She was determined to find out what the Brodies were up to.

She had a range of clothes spread out on the bed so that she could match whatever they appeared in and was therefore presumably appropriate for the destination and activity their prey had in mind. Albert Brodie was on the balcony of his chalet, which conveniently just projected into Carolines's line of sight, writing in a stiff covered note book; the type which used to be called a common place book. His head was down and he wrote painstakingly and slowly occasionally stopping and making more extravagant gestures with his pen. Caroline guessed he was sketching. She focussed the binoculars on Brodie but could not see the sketch pad clearly. She decided she wanted to see that notebook so she hurriedly dressed then walked up the hill away from the Brodie chalet. Shortly she turned downhill but this time keeping as deep into the bushes as she could. She found a large dense shrub about twelve metres away from and directly above the chalet. She could not now see the balcony. The ideal place to view the mysterious book with binoculars was on an open area of lawn.

She looked about and turned over ideas in her mind. Where was Mabel she asked herself. If she was either in the kitchen or the bedroom she was at the back of the house. She crept towards the chalet and rapped smartly on the bedroom window and dashed round the corner of the building. She heard nothing. She waited then, now terrified, repeated the performance. This time she heard a stirring. Then silence again. For the third time she knocked on the window. This time she heard Mabel shout for Albert. Caroline gave enough time for the grumbling man to get to the bedroom and hurried round to the balcony. She jumped up the two steps, took a look at the book which was open just where he had been writing and on the page she saw a drawing of the now familiar crypt. She took a quick look and bolted. As she did the Brodies emerged on to the balcony. Caroline immediately turned back towards them. 'Were you looking for the woodpecker? I'm afraid I've frightened it away. It was a beauty. Did you get a glimpse of it?'

Mabel looked relieved. 'That's what it was. I thought someone was trying to get into my bedroom.'

Even Albert could not forbear a smile at that thought. 'Surprised that there are woodpeckers here. No trees big enough for them.'

'They were pecking at the woodwork of that shed up there. The old one. Must have some bugs in it.'

'Was it spotted?'

Caroline resisted the temptation to point out that she had spotted it. 'I don't know. It had green on the wings.'

'Sounds like the great woodpecker. They're pretty. We must watch out for it, Mabel.'

'I dashed in for my binoculars. That must have frightened it away.'

'Well, not a day for dashing. This is a very restful place isn't it?'

Caroline kept the small talk going for a few minutes in the hope that they might ask her to join them for a drink or something but no such offer was made. So that heart stopping foray achieved nothing.

Caroline lay back and tried to forget the whole missing person business. The late afternoon sun was pleasantly warm and the whole resort seemed quiet and deserted; even the birds were not to be heard. She lay there half asleep and the worries receded. She thought she could hear the sea throwing itself gently on the shore although the beach was half a mile away. She dreamt fitfully of home; of food; of past holidays and of a motor bike. The incongruity of the latter dream startled her and she was awake. She heard the bike - Raoul's bike. The sound faded with a last gentle putter some distance away as always. Sleep would not return. She decided a gentle stroll would be good for her and at the same time settle her curiosity. Where did Raoul leave his bike when he visited whoever he visited.

Leaving the now sleeping Lance she did not change but slipped into her tennis shoes and strolled with an air of nonchalance down in the direction of the village. When she reached the gate and glanced back she could see that Raoul was entering the reception block. Continuing down the only road to the village she was surprised to find no sign of a bike. The road was skirted on one side by a gentle hill sloping upwards and covered in low Myrtle bushes and wild flowers; no cover there for the bike. On the side she was on there was a fence three feet high bordering a field of cork trees. She stopped and stared at the indecently stripped, red trunks of the regularly spaced out trees. They looked biblically old and gnarled. Turning back to her task she could see no gate or entrance of any kind right down to where the fence turned to run parallel to the sea; a long way past where she estimated the sound must have petered out.

She was now so near the village she carried on. She saw the colourful display in the window of the Bleriot Patisserie and decided to go in and buy a gooey cake for Lance. She disapproved of his self indulgent sweet tooth - but it was their holiday. She felt tolerant and virtuous as she walked back up the hill. Some time afterwards Lance reappeared having come up in the bus. He had a bag with the Patisserie shop name on it. Decorated, of course, with little coloured antique airplanes.

Caroline took the bag from him and slipped it into the fridge, put on the kettle and a few minutes later presented Lance with a cup of tea and one of the chestnut fudge patisserie which she had bought. He looked at it in amazement, shook his head, sunk his teeth into the delicacy and leant back with a smile on his face.

'Well. Have a nice rest?'

'No.' Caroline explained her restlessness and the little mystery she had unfolded. Lance had no ideas, only confirmed from his recollection that there was indeed no way off the road. He then told Caroline that he had wakened just in time to follow the Brodies, who had separated as they entered the village. He had decided to follow Albert who had gone directly to the local undertaker and spent an hour there.

'Luckily there was a coffee shop opposite. If it had been any other sort of business I might have gone in on some pretext but I couldn't think of anything to ask for in an undertaker's.'

'So, is he tidying up what has already been done or is there some fresh mischief afoot?'

'I don't know. But I could now recognise both of the undertaker's vehicles and, I think, most of his staff if I ever see them again. When Brodie came out there was a man with him who locked the door behind him so I think that he was probably the boss. What would you call him — the overseer at the undertaker's.'

'You've had too many coffees.'

Lance smiled and continued. 'A large solemn faced man. He would be Monsieur Rivale if the business is still in the family name. They shook hands very formally and went off in opposite directions. By the comings and goings I figure there is a body in there for the night.'

'That wouldn't be unusual. Did it advertise a - what do they call it - a parlour?'

'Yes. I think so. So. It's normal and anyway we can't check up on every corpse that passes through every undertaker.'

'I gather from the small ads that Rivale's is the only undertaker in town. But I take your point. Even with only one we cannot possibly check all its passing trade.'

'No, but perhaps in view of Brodie's visit today tonight's batch might be worth a look.'

'You seemed to have strengthened your resolve. What's done that.'

'This delicious cake. Always feel better after a nice bun. And the whole ghoulish business of watching a funeral parlour for hours made me feel all the more angry that a girl like Jean should be killed. She was too lovely to kill.'

'No one deserves to be killed like that. Lovely or not - surely.'

'Of course. But it seems to highlight the wickedness - the waste. Like a beautiful flower being trampled in full bloom. You don't feel so bad when you tread on a daisy. And all these mourners going in. I kept thinking that no one is paying last respects to poor Jean. So – yes, I do feel more determined now. So let's tell Jean about our quarry, then we can discuss what to do. Some real action.'

Jean was dressed in colourful holiday gear for the first time since she had arrived. Sun glasses made it even more difficult than usual to guess what she was thinking. She thanked them for their information but seemed preoccupied and did not detain them long.

Lance looked troubled as they left her. 'She didn't seem to be paying much attention to us. I think she's a worried woman. I wish she would share her worries with us.'

'I doubt if she'd be allowed to. I think we're already in deeper than they would wish.'

'She seems nervous. As if she is in danger. Her left eye kept twitching. Did you notice?' Caroline nodded.

'Must be tough for a girl.'

'Don't be patronising. A girl can take this just as well as - a boy.'

'Sorry. This boy couldn't take it. I am sure if they, whoever they are, got rid of number one they could just as callously get rid of number two. She has every right to be jumpy. Perhaps we should be watching her back as well.'

'And anyone who seemed to be threatening her would almost certainly have been implicated in Jean One's death. I'm sure she would feel better if she knew we were keeping on eye on her. She has a lonely job.'

'It means we'll have to split up more. As we did just now. We can't keep a track of all this lot otherwise.'

'If we agree to go on with this. I think we have to commit ourselves totally or forget it. Another four eyes certainly seem to be needed.'

'Not just that. We're both bright. We can bring a different perspective to all this. But I do agree it's all or nothing. And I'm ashamed to say I'm getting a kick from this - better than just lying in the sun. But I do agree it is all or nothing.'

'And no one else is bothering about what happened to poor Jean. I would never forget Jean One if we just walked away.'

'Too much sun is bad for you anyway.'

'If the Good Lord had intended us to sun bathe, we would have been born naked.'

'Agreed then. We go for it - as they say nowadays.'

'Agreed.'

They laughed and embraced self consciously.

The idea of breaking into a funeral parlour to look at another corpse did not appeal to them. However they looked at the local papers and it was not too difficult to find out that the only body likely to be at the undertakers officially was a lady in her seventies called Monique Duval. Burials took place soon after death in this hot climate so it was unlikely any others would be still there.

'When you were watching did you see any mourners go in?' asked Caroline.

'Yes, why?'

'How were they dressed?'

'Very few in black. No. Men in white shirts. No tie. Some with sleeves rolled up. Quite informal.'

'And ladies?'

'Dresses. Some colourful and some dull but all dresses. No slacks or shorts. These were just visitors of course not people setting off for a funeral. People paying their last respects I would imagine.'

'Right, one or both of us should pay our fond farewell to the deceased. It's a long shot but if Brodie was there yesterday, you never know, we might learn something.'

'So, who has the best wardrobe for it? Something non touristy.'

'I have the suit I travelled in.'

'Too smart.'

'Thank you darling. That the nicest thing you've said all holiday.'

'How about that green dress?'

'And what's wrong with the green dress? You've never liked that dress have you?' Caroline sounded piqued. Probably because she had always been a bit uncertain herself about the garment in question.

'The green dress is lovely. It's just more - peasant looking.'

'Thanks a bunch. I'll never wear it again now.'

'After this.'

They discussed Lance's wardrobe and they agreed he had nothing remotely suitable so Caroline and the green dress it was for the funeral parlour.

CHAPTER NINE

Lance lay in the maquis on the road down from the Villamaquis. It was half past five and the night dew had not yet been drawn up by the sun. He sneezed and almost choked trying to silence himself but there was no-one within half a mile who could have heard. He was not listening too intently as he knew the noise he was waiting for would be unmistakable. He had erred on the safe side in the time of his arrival or, to put it more accurately, Caroline had erred on the safe side in the time of his arrival. He cursed her silently which, he had learned over the years, was the safest way to curse her.

'Don't get blood on your nice clean shirt,' she had shouted after him from the bed as he left.

After almost half an hour of this, with cramp starting to twitch his legs, he heard the phut-phut of Raoul's bike in the distance. The weak sound, not at all in keeping with the rider, came steadily nearer. Lance raised himself as far as he dare up out of the myrtle and lavender bushes desperately stifling another sneeze. The bike came into sight struggling up the hill with its massive load. It farted gently then stopped.

Raoul bent over the bike and gripped it. Lance blinked in amazement as the big man lifted it high over his head as if it were a pedal cycle and lowered it over the fence into a dense clump of bushes by the side of the cork tree field. He strode off up the hill and Lance, now standing up, could see him enter Villamaquis and skirt up inside the fence and out of sight. He reappeared briefly higher up, still near the fence and climbing up towards the crest of the hill. Lance massaged his legs and limped the first part of the climb back up the road to the villas. Gradually the sun and the exercise loosened his aching limbs.

After breakfast that morning he took a walk up the hill, where he had seen Raoul earlier, starting from the gates of Villamaquis and keeping inside the compound on paths as near to the fence as he could. The only buildings he could find above where he last spied Raoul was the large bungalow, which they had heard was occupied by the sisters, and a huge round water tower.

He went as near as he could to the bungalow and saw that it was constructed almost as two houses but with a linking part too deep to be a passage. It looked as if the occupants shared a lounge or dining room. He could glimpse a maid working away but of Raoul or the sisters he could see nothing. Disappointed, he turned down the hill, now watching more warily then ever for the mighty man who could handle a motor bike like a toy.

When he returned to their chalet Caroline was gone. He went to the breakfast verandah and found only Kirsty sitting alone among the debris of the recently busy table. Kirsty commented that Caroline had left a few minutes ago in a lovely green dress.

Lance braced himself for his next assignment and entered the reception area reluctantly. He was going to sound like a cheap skate which was not at all how he saw himself. A young Corsican girl rose from her desk and enquired how she could assist him. She had the set Villamaquis smile; which was, however, more genuine than most holiday smiles.

'Good morning, miss. I would like to pay for the drinks I've had so far. I don't like to let the account run up. Like to know what spending money I'm going to have at the end of the holiday. You know - for presents and things. I would have calculated it myself but the book has been replaced. Old one finished is it?'

'No. Someone spilled fruit juice all over the last one. Horrible sticky mess. But I think we can work it out if these pages have not been affected. Give me a couple of minutes.'

She returned in three minutes. 'Your account comes to one hundred and forty three euros. Or do you wish to pay in sterling?'

'No, euros will do fine.' He handed over the money, thanked her and made his way to the bar to think. He now knew that the original book still survived but he did not know how to get at the desired volume or why the spoiler had not just stolen the book.

As soon as he went to sign for a whisky he had helped himself to, he chose an alcoholic drink so that he could sign with authenticity, he saw why the book had not been stolen. It was a hard bound book chained to the wall with a padlock. The trust implied in the word courtesy did not apparently extend to allowing people to make off with the book after a week of hearty drinking.

He sipped his whisky and for a moment the strong familiar taste made him feel homesick and disheartened, then he looked at the book and thought of Jean One signing for her refreshing orange juice that hot and fateful afternoon and his anger and resolve returned.

An examination of the previous pages confirmed that the new book started just after Caroline had signed for her drinks. 'Did this mean that Caroline had inadvertantly alerted someone who was covering their tracks?' He then looked at the other signatures. Jean Two had signed several times, always for a brandy. The signature bore no resemblance to the writing on the luggage labels.

Caroline was indeed wearing the soon to be discarded green dress as she headed towards the village. A head scarf fashioned from a sun top covered her gleaming brown hair. She had rubbed her eyes with make up mixed with lipstick and looked as if she had spent the last twenty four hours in tears. As she left the chalet she felt just right for the task ahead particularly when she passed Ross and didn't get a glimmer of recognition.

As she entered the shadowed front room of the undertaker's premises her confidence slipped away. Her smart shoes had clicked noisily on the pavement and she had forced herself to step boldly through the door so that her noisy entrance would attract immediate attention but the heavy carpet, the first she had walked on for a week, deadened all sound of her entry. The room was empty and no one came to greet her so she took the unwelcome opportunity to have a careful look round. The room was dull yet dignified. There were flowers around the room and Caroline's instinct to check if they were artificial was frustrated by glass covers. The only other decorations were artistically printed notices outlining the various services offered and an ornate cross. She noticed a bell push on a counter and after a moments hesitation she pushed it. Instead of the buzz just under her finger she had been expecting a faint growl came from beyond a screened door, as if someone in there was protesting at the interruption. She almost fled.

Before she could even turn the screen parted and a large, mild looking, middle aged man with a set sympathetic look set on his face floated noiselessly into the room.

'Monique est ici?' Caroline croaked out the question before the man could say a word, which she would most certainly not have understood. She added a little choked sob.

'Oui, Madam.'

'Puis-je?' She put her hand up to her eyes and turned towards the inner door.

The man held back the screen and beckoned her through. He nodded towards a coffin and as Caroline walked towards it head bowed he paused and watched her carefully then shuffled backwards through a door which led further into the premises. Again she had a look round. There was only one coffin in the room. It was on a raised dais and it was open. She started to take a deep breath, decided that wasn't a good idea, braced herself and looked down at the recently expired Monique. There lay an elderly lady with a serene look on her face: her lack of deathly pallor confused Caroline. She turned away; the closed eyes seemed a token of reproach. Sobbing loudly in the hope that this would give her a little more time she took a closer look at the room. It revealed no surprises; bare panelled walls, neutral carpet and a few flowers. After a short interval she knocked at the inner door and pushed it open. She could see nothing but a small, untidy office. An old lady had her head down over some papers. The undertaker hurried over and indicated that she should go the other way. Caroline turned away and, sobbing and apologising, hurried out through the room where the coffin lay.

After scrubbing the masking material off her face Caroline walked with Lance down to the stones seats which seemed to have some importance in the mystery. Once settled she reported to Lance.

'A dear old lady - and by herself. She looked so peaceful, Lance. A long and happy life I would guess.'

'Good for her.' Lance sounded bitter.

'You know as I was coming out I think I saw the name Albert Brodie on a business card in one of those little wall racks. There were lots there but mostly old and faded. Been there for donkeys. His stood out.'

'Well, we knew he had been there. However. Process of elimination. We now know he didn't leave a body.'

'We also now know that it is not too difficult for an unauthorised person to get into the parlour.'

'And if they had a body slung over their shoulder it could have been slipped into the coffin unnoticed.'

'Don't be sarcastic.' Caroline was not in the mood for that.

'But say two mourners went in but only one came out. You said you were left alone. Then the person left could hide till night time then let another in who might have our body.'

'You should see the inside of that place. The only place you could hide was in the coffin and I refuse even to think of that again. We're not playing musical boxes.'

'Was the pedestal thing hollow?' asked Lance.

'I don't know.'

'Something to think about.'

'I'll add it to my notes.'

'Was it a solid oak coffin?'

'I don't think so. More a mahogany colour.'

'So they don't all get the top quality coffin. Interesting. What did Brodie want there? And how do we find out? We can't follow the undertaker as well.'

'No, but we could follow the funeral procession tomorrow. Find out how close it passes to this place for a start. This is where Raoul dumps his bike. And it must be very near where Donna told us he helped with the coffin. Check how the box is conveyed. Could there have been two bodies in the Fournier coffin en route? What else could we find out? Nothing probably. Oh, what was Raoul doing giving a helping hand? Anyway somewhere, somehow we think an extra body was put in. If that did happen we must find out where and how. Perhaps right here.' Caroline shuddered.

'And, of course who.' added Lance.

The younger guests left the dinner table early that night and Meryl told Caroline that there would be a band from France at the poolside in the evening. Evidently it was very popular, played accordion music, even the older guests liked it she informed them helpfully.

In spite of being put off by that remark Lance and Caroline found themselves drawn towards the music which was indeed melodious, and not too loud. Extra tables and chairs had been laid out. The three piece band was playing familiar sounding tunes. A few couples were dancing. They sat down, not too near the musicians. The found that there was a bottle of white wine and a bottle of red wine on their, and every other, table.

After two glasses of the gratuitous grape Lance was thinking perhaps he should take his wife up to dance when the Frenchman appeared at her elbow. He looked first at Lance who shrugged and then at Caroline who rose to her feet hesitantly. She enjoyed dancing but she preferred that her partner could also dance.

She was soon reassured on that score as they glided smoothly round the small raised wooden floor. The music was lovely, the night was warm and her partner could dance. She relaxed and closed her eyes. They dance closely and gracefully. He could dance. His grip gradually tightened. Yes, he had danced before.

'It's getting hot,' whispered Caroline.

His grip slackened almost imperceptibly. 'You dance beautifully.' He murmured.

'And you.'

'You have grace - - . Sorry, what is your name?'

'Caroline.'

'What a pretty name. Musical.'

'Yes, Christmas music.'

'That is a coincidence. I am Christophe.'

'You are French?'

'I am but I live here now.'

'It is a lovely island.'

His cheek came a little closer to hers. She turned her face straight at him and spoke. 'It is a beautiful night.'

He was silent for a time, his hands moving gently on her back. 'You can learn a lot about a woman as you dance with her.'

'You mean you can tell what your prospects are.'

Christophe now laughed and loosened his hold on her still more and they danced silently until the music stopped.

As they sat sipping the wine and watching the dancers Caroline wondered what Christophe had learned about her as they danced. He did not ask her to dance again.

CHAPTER TEN

The funeral of Monique Rivale was a poorly attended affair as is often the case with the elderly many of whose friends have predeceased them. Thus Caroline's presence was conspicuous but welcome. The few other mourners smiled at her but made no attempt to engage her in conversation. She was pleased about that. They seemed to have come in pairs and whispered to each other non stop as if they had not met for a long time, perhaps since the last family funeral. There was a brief service at the parlour during which she and Monsieur Duval exchanged sympathetic smiles of recognition. The coffin was then carried by the undertaker and his assistant into a stately but very old limousine which then proceeded slowly towards the graveyard. The mourners followed on foot.

The procession stopped on the road up to the Villamaquis. There the coffin was removed from the car and laid on two stones set back in the pavement; about two feet high and parallel. Caroline recognised them as their regular stopping place on their way up the hill when they walked back from the village and where they had sat the previous day; so convenient, just half way up. They had relaxed several times where the coffin now rested, holding hands, recovering their breath and admiring the view. It seemed so irreverent now. Lance observing the group from afar recognised the spot as being very near to where Raoul had dumped his bike that morning.

Unseen to all but the most attentive observer, in which category Caroline most definitely placed herself, the gentlemen in black coats all took a stealthy quaff from small bottles extracted from deep in the dark folds of their garments. One of them was thrown into paroxisms of discomfort and embarrassment when his fortifying brew went down the wrong way. The ladies looked scornful; the word 'men' illuminated briefly on their lined, lived in faces. In French, of course. The coffin was now lifted by four pall bearers who crossed the road into the maquis opposite and proceeded unsteadily up a path which had not been apparent till then. She wondered if this lot would have been struggling with more weight. They certainly set off with a jaunty enough stride after the rest and the refreshment. In such circumstances it would be reasonable to bank on them not noticing any extra weight particularly as it was probably at this stage that the mourners had to bear the burden of the casket on its last journey for the first time. Caroline soon realised that they were heading for the graveyard but approaching it from the opposite direction. Although the procession was slow they reached the cemetery in less than half the time it took Lance and Caroline on their respective visits. That this was the traditional route was confirmed by the presence at intervals of further blocks on which to rest the melancholy load. Shortly after entering the tree lined avenues the coffin was rested outside a sad, neglected looking crypt. Another short service mumbled in French to the small group then the body was taken inside the crypt. As they left, Caroline noticed workmen approaching to seal it off. She decided not to accompany the mourners back to the village and face the possible embarrassing offer of hospitality so she slunk into the trees and let them get well away before she started back.

Lance and Caroline arrived at the dining table early to quiz the girls. They had decided it was better to do this informally with both girls present than to appear too intense and interested. The meal was not ready but the girls were going in and out with dishes.

'You're early.' Donna brought out a tray of glasses.

'I came along to chat up you girls - and my wife came to stop me.'

'We thought it was later. Do you mind?' asked Caroline.

'Not at all. The scent of our delicious concoction will get your juices going.'

'I've been hoping for that all holiday. Hasn't it been another lovely day?' He waited until Donna was close to him. 'We had a most enjoyable walk about the village. Fascinating. It's so interesting to see how other people live. Not so different really. Except, I suppose everyone adapts to the heat. But we did see one strange thing. Can you throw any light on it, Donna. Coming up the road we saw a coffin rested on some stone seats by the way side. The mourners seem to be taking a break. Looked most odd.'

'I saw an old crone leave here seriously dressed. Must have been that funeral. I couldn't make out who it was. One of the cleaning staff probably.'

Lance shot a beaming smile at a put-out looking Caroline.

Donna continued 'Oh, they all stop at that spot. Traditional. They always carry the coffin the last half mile. Shows deference they say.'

From the kitchen Meryl shouted out. 'Some have a wee drink at that stage. A toast to show their respect or is it a wee snort to give them strength for the hill.'

'It certainly looks a fair climb and some of the pall bearers didn't look too young.' Caroline looked sympathetic.

'That'll be where the men you told us about stumbled - when Raoul took over - was it?' asked Lance.

'That's right,' shouted Donna.

'Stumbled my foot,' interrupter Meryl. 'I heard the real story. They were evidently just lifting the box to start up the hill and having a bit of a struggle, probably too much to drink, when a sun bather rose out of the maquis on the other side of the road. Not a stitch on. I think the old boys carrying the box were overcome. They probably hadn't seen a naked woman for half a century.' Lance grimaced at the ready assumption by the young that no one over thirty or thereabouts experienced such delights. Meryl laughed at his expression. 'The women in the procession shouted at the sun bather who evidently took some time to realise what was going on. I thought at one stage the old boys were going to chase her. Then she grabbed her clothes and fled. By that time it was a complete shambles so big Roaul who was passing took one end of the box and they headed up the hill; the men in the party kept looking back and stumbling all over the place as they headed for the cemetery. Must have been a laugh.'

Lance and Caroline forced out a chuckle.

'Yes. I can just imagine Jacques Tati in that scene,' commented Caroline.

While the girls were laying the table a group of four men walked in the direction of one of the other dining chalets.

'Who are they, Meryl? I've seen them about. They dress like they were on holiday but they don't look very merry.'

'They're locals. The sisters always keep a few places for Corsicans. They're probably wishing they were in Rimini or Marbella.'

'Or Blackpool,' suggested Caroline.

Lance and Caroline had time before the others arrived to agree that a visit to the resting stones was called for. The girls disappeared into the kitchen. So left by themselves they discussed whether the latest information added to the progress they were making. They agreed they still understood very little of what was going on around them. Nothing fitted.

'Tomorrow the resting stones, but what about tonight? We're wasting time. The trail will go cold on us.' Caroline tried to banish from her mine the thought of the body which would already be cold. 'What can we do tonight?'

'Ross. Our correlation. His absence at breakfast. Where does he go every second night – when the plane arrives in the morning? He might lead us somewhere.'

'He seems a nice lad,' protested Caroline.

'But money. He said he would do anything for money.'

'Oh, I hope he hasn't got into something dreadful. Once you start on the slippery slope, you're stuck.'

'That sounds right. Well, let's follow him tonight. Have the car at the ready. We might have to chase him.' Lance's eyes widened and a boyish expression of anticipation lit up his face.

'Forget the Bond bit. Over sixty and I am getting out.'

'Spoil sport. Listen – you leave the table first. Say you have a headache.'

'Funny you should say that. I was planning to have a headache tonight.'

'Very droll. OK. You watch from a vantage point in the garden when he leaves the table then I'll come to the chalet and we will take it from there.'

They did that. When Lance returned to the chalet Caroline was waiting impatiently.

'He's gone to his chalet. As far as I know he hasn't come out yet. Not by the usual path anyway.'

Lance slipped on a warm jerkin. 'I'll go and have a look. I'll come back for you if I can but if he makes a dash for it I'll follow him myself. See you.'

He left and turned along past the dining chalet where the girls were clearing up. He exchanged a few pleasantries with them and walked towards the chalet occupied by Ross and Ian. The light was on and Ross was sitting on the balcony. The young man looked round from time to time. Ian came out and walked towards the little bus but Ross stayed where he was.

'He is waiting for a signal,' thought Lance, skulking self consciously among the trees.

It was suddenly darker and he realised the light had gone out in the dining chalet. Ross rose. The bathroom light went on. Lance was able to see the young man comb his hair. Two minutes later he came out and strode down the hill.

'Well,' Caroline stood up and reached for her jacket. 'Are we off?'
'No. I've cracked it all by myself.' Lance smirked.
'Go on.'
'The correlation.'
'Yes. The plane. So?'
'There's another correlation.' He lingered teasingly and Caroline waited.
'Donna is not on duty for breakfast every second day.'
They collapsed into each others arms laughing. Caroline forgot the threatened headache.

It was an early start. Caroline hid herself among the bushes up the hill near to the sisters' house. She was to observe exactly what Raoul did when he arrived early in the morning. Meantime, and this was what really necessitated the crack of dawn raid, Lance would have a look at the place Raoul hid his bike. They thought it would be safe then as the timing of his movements did not vary. Lance had also given very long and careful thought as to the safest place from which to make his observations. Having seen the man lift the bike so effortlessly he did not wish to cross Raoul or his path.

Caroline shivered in the shadows of some tall cypress trees only the cold keeping her awake in the dawn light. She lay on a travelling rug she had thoughtfully provided for herself and had hidden from the potentially envious eyes of her spouse; they had only brought one. She was listening carefully as she realised that there would be a period of silence after Raoul abandoned the bike. She had calculated that it would take him around four minutes to get to her. She looked at her watch twenty times in that four minutes.

He was right on time. He came up the hill walking close by the fence although there was no proper path there. Caroline had seen the security man take the same rough route. However Raoul did not have the same bored lack of expression of the average security man. He positively bristled as if expecting something to happen and he looked as if he were ready for it. When he drew almost level with the bungalow he crouched further down and carried on round to the back of the house. Caroline cursed inwardly. She had placed herself with a perfect view of both front entrances. She groaned as she straightened herself. She hurried round to the back of the house just in time to see a door open and the large man disappear inside.

She desperately hoped he would not be too long; it was still cold in the shadows. To her great relief the door opened again within five minutes. Raoul came out flexing his great fingers.

Caroline was just near enough to hear a female voice whispering, 'No, Raoul. That would be the end of us. Put all thoughts of killing out of your mind. Promise.' There was no response. The plea was repeated earnestly. 'Promise.'

Raoul turned, spread his huge hands, shrugged and gave the tiniest nod of his head. He hurried down passing within ten feet of the petrified Caroline. She kept watch for some time longer. The two wings of the house were well hidden but the connecting part had large windows and it was not long before she saw the sisters meet and sit at the breakfast table. A young lady served them. Significantly - she hoped - she noted that Rhoda came from the wing into which Raoul had been so obviously expected and welcomed. She also noted that Raoul's departure followed immediately on Rona's bedroom light going on.

Lance also, exactly as anticipated, heard the sound of the bike far down the hill not long after they had taken up their respective positions. Lance reflected that he could well be lying on the same spot as the naked sunbather but it was far too early in the morning to be excited by such thoughts. He did however look around for signs of any previous occupant in case it might ever be relevant and also to add credibility to Meryl's fanciful sounding tale. There was indeed a slightly flattened spot but the undergrowth was rough and jagged. Not an ideal place for sunbathing. There was also a very pleasant perfume but he soon worked out by its pervasiveness that it was from the maquis and not a trace of the departed lady.

In spite of having witnessed it before Lance could not help marvelling as the big man effortlessly swung the bike over the fence and strode off up the hill. As soon as he was out of sight Lance mentally handed him over to Caroline, darted across the road and climbed the fence. The thicket into which the bike had been gently lowered stretched about twelve feet in each direction with lower growth in the centre. The bike nestled in the middle quite hidden even from someone passing two feet away. There were oil stains on the ground in the centre of the bush confirming that this was a regular hiding place for the bike. Lance noticed the bike was not even padlocked.

He looked back over the fence and saw that the resting stones were only ten yards away close into the fence on what passed for a pavement. Staying inside the fence he crept along until he was right opposite the stones.

He looked closely at them and could see nothing of particular interest. He turned inwards and now he saw that the grass was beaten down just in from the twin stones. He also saw that, looking up the slight incline towards the Villamaquis there were signs of flattened grass and broken twigs among the low bushes. His heart pounding he followed the tracks upwards.

Several times he lost the trail but circling around as he had seen red indians do in old movies he picked up the line of disturbed foliage. After about three hundred yards of this he was at the perimeter of the Villamaquis. Again there was a disturbed patch but he could see nothing that gave any hint of how a body could have been taken over the high boundary fence.

The starting of the bike engine made him drop to the ground but he was well out of sight of Raoul. He waited till the sound passed then faded before hurrying back. He knew that he had made an important discovery. The resting stones played a significant part in the gruesome mystery.

CHAPTER ELEVEN

They basked for a while, wearing only their bathrobes, in the gentle heat of the rising sun before getting ready for breakfast. They shared a hot shower and this put Lance in a good mood; too good Caroline thought and turned the control quickly to cold. They exchanged notes as they dressed and agreed they had another few pieces of the jigsaw in place.

Caroline's account of the brief overheard conversation between Raoul and Rhoda was even more effective than the cold shower. They both avoided discussing short listing the possible intended victims in the fear that they might have to list themselves. They merely shared the hope that Rhoda had a strong influence on the aspiring killer.

Before they had arrived the others had been discussing a picnic. Evidently the girls were free to prepare such a picnic instead of dinner but only if all the group wished it. It seemed there were five enthusiasts, one doubtful and they were waiting for the Lockhart votes. Ross was just turning round Jean Two with the remark. 'You are on holiday you know.' Which, as Lance and Caroline knew, was exactly the impression she wished to create. As soon as Caroline said yes Jean acquiesced. It was left to the girls to choose the site.

Now, in the hope of discovering more pieces for the jigsaw, Caroline channelled the conversation on to the sisters.

'I hear everyone call them the Corsican Sisters. I was surprised when they spoke with an English accent,' remarked Caroline.

'There was a literary gent here last year who kept calling them that and it just stuck. They've been here such a long time they look native,' Donna explained with no reference to the Corsican Brothers and added that the two ladies, then quite young, had come out as couriers with a travel company. The sisters had been outraged by the way the customers were treated and thought they could do better and made up their minds to try. They so objected to their employers herding the clients about like cattle that they choose as their guiding principle the freedom of the holiday makers to do whatever they chose. The result had been a very happy, occasionally outrageous --

'And,' Meryl added emphatically, 'I'm sure, very profitable business.'

'They look as if they must have been good looking women in their time.' Lance looked around for confirmation. 'Neither of them ever get married?'

'No, I don't think so. I don't think Mona is that way inclined. I think she has had a bad experience.'

'Haven't we all,' quipped Caroline.

Meryl laughed and continued, 'But I've seen Rhoda looking at the talent in the swimming pool. Not entirely disinterested I would say.'

Ross looked at Donna. 'This place must keep them very busy, keeping an idle staff like this up to scratch.'

Donna flicked a corn flake at him. It was swooped on by a tiny colourful bird.

'They work us very hard,' protested Donna, 'but they treat us well provided everything is done their way. Meryl and I are lucky. They normally won't employ anyone with any experience in the tourist trade. They think they'll bring bad habits.'

'They do.' quipped Ross as he rose and left the table.

'Freedom to be rude to the serving wenches is not included,' shouted Donna after him.

Albert Brodie was looking on with a slightly bewildered expression on his face. 'You don't get much courtesy from the young these days.'

'He's just joking,' growled Mabel sotto voce.

'It's O K Mister Brodie. I can look after myself. I had three brothers. All worse than that.'

'How nice for you.' Albert looked sad. 'I had no brothers or sisters.' He picked up a plastic sugar shaker and looked scornfully at it. 'Same shape as our silver one at home,' he remarked to Mabel and to everyone.

'The sisters do employ some strange people. Big Raoul for instance. He seems to be out of place here but I get the impression that he and Rhoda get on well.' Lance was trying hard to get the conversation back onto his rails.

Jean Two looked hard at him. 'What gave you that impression?'

'Not much really. He seems to visit her quite a lot and comes away with a smile on his face.' Lance himself smiled.

'Probably being paid.' Donna tried to look cynical.

'Not that kind of smile.'

'Pay no attention to him Donna. Lance looks for romance everywhere.' Caroline looked indulgently at her husband.

'And very rarely finds it.' Lance reposted with his boyish grin.

Lance's next suggestion implied that they kill two birds, although he did not use that expression. They would visit Sartene and look at the three crypts Caroline had noted as having attracted Brodie's close attention. They could also sample the restaurant commended by Donna which they had been cheated out of visiting on their last visit.

They enjoyed again the approach to this ancient town where earlier man had tried to outdo the precipitous cliffs with his soaring granite buildings; the cold grey contrasting with the warm orange of the hills. Thus, in the searing heat up in the thin mountain air it was always possible to find shade; the high houses were huddled close together creating dark cool passages. Many arches and bridges linked the buildings at all levels creating more pleasant shadows.

They visited the crypts and examined them closely but there were no signs that they had been disturbed. They had to admit, in spite of their recently formed antipathy to such places, that they were each beautiful in their own way.

They would not have been surprised to see other guests from the Villamaquis in the commended restaurant as there was a notice advertising the attractions of the town at the villas and it was highlighted, but they were surprised to see the bus driver. It did not seem his sort of place. Lance recognised his companion as the lady from the café on the road from the airport.

'You know that ridiculous moustache does not look real to me,' whispered Caroline.

'Will I go and give it a tug?'

They sat in the small bar drinking a cool glass of wine; Caroline was going to drive so Lance was not holding back. They waited in unspoken agreement until the others moved to the dining room. The bus driver chose a small booth in which they were not visible to other diners.

Lance and Caroline chose the next booth, happily vacant, and slipped in unnoticed by the now engrossed couple. One of the attractions of the place was the absence of background music and they blessed this fact. They could hear their neighbours.

'It's a nice place. Not my style but a nice place.' The bus driver was speaking French but they were speaking slowly as if making allowances for each other's dialect so the Lockharts were able to pick up the gist easily, if not all the words. 'So, you want to buy it. Buy it.'

'She does not want to sell.'

'So what? You know the big men. The land owners. They will put her out.'

'I'm sure. But it would cost a lot. Perhaps too much.'

'But you are making a fortune since I got you the Villamaquis business.'

'Not a fortune. I could raise the price.'

'Not yet. I have influence on Mona but she has limits. And I have another favour to ask her. Besides that she has Rhoda to convince. Leave it a little while.'

'I don't understand how you get Mona to listen to you at all.'

'Ah, many women listen to me. I wish I could count on you as one of them.' They heard the bus driver slurp his soup.

'I am looking for a man who would be at home in a place like this.'

'Suit yourself. I can find women.'

The café proprietor's response was obviously a colloquial expression. They could not understand it. They missed the next part of the conversation as the waitress took their order. When she had gone the others were eating in silence.

Shortly afterwards they rose to leave and as they passed Lance and Caroline heard the driver hiss, 'Remember, you need me.'

As they were heading for the door the woman growled. 'Just you watch Raoul. I don't trust that man. I've worked hard. I don't want a thug ruining my business.'

'Well, what do you make of that?' asked Caroline when the others had passed out of earshot. 'Didn't sound as if that was entirely above board.'

'No. In fact a typical business meeting.'

'You're getting cynical in your old age.'

'Old. I'll show you old when we get on the tennis courts. If we ever do.'

The lunch lived up to their wildest expectations. They lingered and savoured it. The wine, new to them, matched the meal perfectly. The staff were friendly and efficient and appeared happy that the couple were not hurrying. They agreed that it would not enhance the quality of life in the world if the café owner did buy this lovely inn. Their only other worry was the knowledge that they were going back to a fine evening meal cooked by the girls who did not like to see their offerings spurned

They drove down the hill deep in thought. As they walked back to their chalet Lance seized Caroline's sleeve. 'Now, don't just accuse me again of looking for romance everywhere but'--, he nodded towards the Frenchman who was standing by some bushes. 'Do you see who is watching Jean Two closely?'

'Funny you should say that. I've been noticing that he's often near her but not too near. Maybe we're getting jumpy but I think we should watch her back a bit. We don't want to lose two of them.'

'Agreed. But I think this is one bit of information we should give her. She needs a bodyguard.'

They told the policewoman of their fears and she this time seemed to welcome their warning and thanked them warmly but she again repeated her instruction to them to stay out of it. She was not at all enthusiastic about their offer to watch her back

She positively snapped. 'No, don't do that. It would only make me more conspicuous. I have to go to some strange places. You would look out of place. If they heard back home that I had been using civilians all hell would be let loose. Just watch the Brodies. That's all I ask and it's more than I should. If they were involved in Jean's - whatever - they might want to do the same to me.' Seeing their expression on her dismissive way of referring to Jean's death she continued. 'I can not, I'm sorry to say, follow up what happened to my colleague. It may sound hard hearted but I must concentrate on the job I'm here to do. It will maybe all resolve itself when the job is completed. What's done is done and cannot be undone, that's for sure. I've enough to worry about without even thinking about that. Just watch the Brodies for me. Do just that for me and I can cope with the rest. It won't be long now. Just don't get under my feet, whatever you do. Please.' She smiled sweetly and turned away.

They watched her stocky body as she walked off. She strode confidently as she always did, looking as if she know exactly where she was going. She did, however, glance at the Frenchman as she passed and they felt their message had been heeded.

'Funny if she started following him and he was following her. They could end up, up each other's ----'

'That'll do, Lance. Keep your mind on the problem.'

That evening they set off on the picnic. Even the Brodies dressed appropriately for the occasion. Mavis picked an invisible speck from Albert's holiday shirt as if it were a dark business suit. The girls had ruled that no one should drive and had obtained from the sisters the services of the bus driver. Donna explained as they drove along the coast road that they had chosen a place near Filitosa for those who wished to visit that historic site while the girls prepared the open air feast and also because it was near a small bay for those with other tastes.

'And Sollacaro is very near. Someone wrote about it in a book. People go to see it.'

The bus driver turned. 'Dumas. The Corsican Brothers.'

The bus drew up by a stream right by where it ran into the sea. Donna explained which direction was which and asked that they all be back by seven thirty. She opted to stay by the sea until the preparations would have to start and was joined by Meryl, Ian and Ross. The other six decided on Filitosa. The driver stayed by his bus.

Albert grew quite excited as Kirsty told him of some of the treats in store for him. Mabel walked along behind shrugging away. Jean turned into a small museum as the others strode in the direction indicated by the discreet signs. They came soon to a large fortification on the crest of a gentle hill.

'Why do ruins so often look better than new buildings?' asked Lance.

'Natural raw materials I think. Mellows well. And look at the shapes.'

'Accidental art or something. It is lovely. Even the half hidden stones are carved.'

Kirsty chipped in. 'The Torreans used sculptures from the Megalithic people as building materials. Shame really. It would have been nice to have seen both ages represented alongside each other. Uncivilised.'

'Not tolerant to other peoples like our present day civilisations,' said Lance sarcastically.

Kirsty went on unabashed. 'You see some of the carvings show the Torreans wearing helmets with horns yet we are a far way from the Vikings. A bit of a mystery still. And there are some wonderful megalithic statues, or menhirs as they are called, over in that valley. I don't think they are what Ross thought they were and it says nothing about that in this book.'

Just at this moment Albert Brodie called them over to view a sacrificial altar. 'Look,' he shouted, 'this is where the blood must have flowed.' He was looking admiringly at a smoothly chiselled channel carved in the stone. Then his eyes lit on a notice which declared that a skull had been found nearby recently and he hurried off to the museum to see it. Mabel followed leaving the bank of flowers she had been admiring.

Lance and Caroline walked to the top of the hill overlooking the whole site and sat, also enjoying the mass of wild flowers which coloured the hillside and the evening sun which coloured the sky. That this had been a place where people had chosen to live since the stone age seemed perfectly natural to them.

'So pretty and so peaceful,' remarked Caroline lying back in the grass and closing her eyes.

'Isn't it? In a place like this why would they want to sacrifice anyone?'

'How else would people who are our forbears behave?'

'Now, who's the cynic?'

When they passed the museum on the way out Jean two had already gone. They found her back by the bus. The girls were laying out the picnic while the young men were placing the wine bottles in the stream to cool.

All four looked scorched and flushed. Jean was talking earnestly to the bus driver but as they approached she hastily left him and joined the others.

When Meryl declared that all was ready the bus driver also joined them but stayed a little apart and did not take part in the conversation. His eyes followed Lance closely as he walked over to the bus to get Caroline's rug. Lance noticed that the black brief case was chained to the steering wheel. He sat down on the grass absently looking at the skimpily clad Donna.

'What are you doing?' asked Caroline.

'Thinking.'

'Well, in that case is it not your own navel you are supposed to contemplate?'

'Listen, it is a man who has a Degas at home who is going to appreciate a Renoir elsewhere. But seriously, I've been wondering what is in that briefcase that's so important.'

'I have noticed and noted it in my little pad. He does look after it very carefully. He does the banking for the sisters. I wonder if he does the banking for the café as well.'

'Would make sense. No bank out there. I was hoping for a more exotic reason.'

'This is supposed to be a romantic picnic. You concentrate on your exotic wife.'

He did.

They lay quiet and still in that beautiful halfway house between waking and sleeping. It had been a tiring day so it would not have been long before they would have slipped into sleep. Then a dreadful single roar ripped into their ears. Other similar noises, some farther away some even nearer, joined and formed a painful cacophony. The sound surged and faded, welled and dwindled but even at its lowest the sound was ear splittingly loud.

Lance sat up. 'These bloody bikes again.'

'Boys will be boys. Pull the blanket over your head.'

They both did that, but to no avail. The noise penetrated any of the defences they tried.

'It must be some sort of race.'

'At night. In these mountains. They must be mad.'

After a few minutes Lance sat up. 'If you can't beat them join them. I'm going out to watch. I can't sleep. It might even be fun.'

'You're mad too,' declared Caroline, pulling the blankets further over her head and reaching for Lance's as extra insulation.

Lance pulled on his warmest clothing and was about to leave when Caroline sat up. 'I can't stand this. Wait for me. I'll come. Can't be worse than this.'

She pulled on a sweater and trousers over her night wear and followed Lance out to the Volkswagen.

They drove in silence down the hill. That is to say they drove without speaking. The option of silence was not available to them. Lance headed towards the epicentre of the uproar. As they approached the village they saw a large powerful bike with dozens of mirrors come roaring towards them, turn and throb up the hill. Another followed in half a minute.

Lance turned up the same hill keeping hard into the verge. A third bike screamed past, missing them by inches.

'I don't like this,' howled Caroline at the top of her voice.

'Yes, they are good aren't they,' Lance screamed back.

After they had ascended a few hundred feet Lance pulled into a layby with a fine view down the hill.

'We should see the fun from here.'

The next bike to pass pulled further up the road and stopped. The biker turned and faced them, pointing his machine downhill.

'Blown a gasket. I'm not surprised.'

They could now see that the bikes were coming up from the village past them then, using a rough track, cutting across to another road, down again far to the other side of the village and back; a fearsome circuit. They were not all large powerful machines but they were all noisy.

'I don't know much about motor bikes but I don't understand why they go downhill on full throttle.'

'Little boys like making a noise,' scoffed Caroline.

Caroline was now getting chilly and she protested. 'I've had enough of this. Let's go home. By the time we get back they'll have stopped. I hope.'

Lance was easing out of the parking place when the bike which had stopped beyond them leapt to life and hurtled down towards them. The nose of the Volkswagen was about a foot into the roadway when the bike headed straight at it. Lance had pressed the accelerator sharply to come out as fast as he could to ensure that he wasn't going to be straddling the road longer than necessary with all this frantic activity around. As soon as he saw the bike speeding towards him he applied the brakes viciously and turned the wheel downhill, all the time desperately trying to remember which was the safer verge. It was all he could do. He had no time to do more to avoid the bike which now hit him mid on, hard. With a scream of rubber the motor cyclist regained control with great skill, shot across the road and disappeared from sight.

The car now swung violently about under the conflicting pressures of brake, steering wheel, the blow and gravity. It came to a sudden stop with its already thumped side resting hard against a tree which was hanging over the drop steep down into the woods.

They sat trembling. Then Lance spoke unsteadily. 'You all right, darling?' His voice was anxious.

'Yes. Seem to be. I'll check in detail later. You?'

'Fine. We'd better look and see if the idiot cyclist is OK.' Lance climbed out.

'Wait. I can't get out. The door's stuck. Anyway I think I go over the edge if I get out at this side.'

Lance went round to her side. He had difficulty finding a surface to place his feet as the ground dropped steeply so, without leverage, he could not budge the door. There was huge dent just about midships.

'You'll have to come out my door.'

Caroline struggled over the gear lever and brake. Concerned for the cyclist, they looked down where the bike had disappeared. After the initial leap it was not as steep as they had feared. Then they saw the tail light of the bike far below wending its way slowly through the sparse trees.

'Who's a lucky boy? Let's get going if we can. I don't think this is a clever place for the car to be. We could be hit again. I hope we can start. We don't want to have to push with these maniacs about.'

They scrambled into the damaged vehicle and, to their great relief, it started at the third time of asking. Lance reversed carefully away from the tree, scraping the side of the car which had already been stripped of large patches of paint, and set off gingerly down the road. Then to their alarm another bike thundered towards them but it passed within inches and disappeared up the dark road.

'We'll have to report this to the police for the rental people.'

'Did you get the bike's number?'

Lance shook his head. 'You know, now you mention it I don't think any of them were showing numbers. Weird.'

CHAPTER TWELVE

Next morning they felt impotent and vulnerable without transport so, as soon as they had breakfast, they took the wounded car down to the village to have it replaced. First they drove to the police station to report the incident. On the way Lance noticed that the petrol gauge was at zero. They stopped at a petrol station but could not get into the petrol tank as the cap had been damaged in the collision. It was distorted and jammed. They free wheeled on down with their fingers crossed.

Lance forced a smile. 'I now know why they call this car the Polo. It's the car with the hole in the middle.'

They made it. The police were not too interested and gave them a certificate certifying that the accident had been reported. Luckily the rental firm was almost next door. When they saw the police paperwork the rental people were equally sanguine about it all and gave them another car. The matter of fact way that the rental clerk accepted their story did nothing to reassure Lance about the safely of the roads in the area. They drove back to Villamaquis and decided to do no more driving today if possible.

'You sounded a bit of a Charlie explaining all that to the police. No conviction. If that's the right way of putting it?'

'Strange you should say that. I was half way through my little spiel when I realised that we were almost certainly hit deliberately. Whatever they were up to they didn't want spectators.'

They had found that a seat near the pool was the best place to watch passing traffic. Most of the holiday makers walked this way whether to the pool itself, the reception, the bar or to the gate. The little bus stopped within sight. Also it was an unremarkable place to be sitting. A few holidaymakers were resting by the pool after the exertion of eating a breakfast.

It was quiet and they were half dozing in the pleasant shade. The only disturbance was when Ian and Ross shouted to them as they passed noisily. They were discussing their intentions. Ross was going to wait at the gate for Raoul and Ian apparently had a tryst on the beach.

As they parted Ross shouted 'Be good, she's a nice girl.'

'Chance would be a fine thing,' retorted Ian.

Shortly after that they heard the unmistakable sound of Raoul's bike. It stopped briefly and then the sound diminished as it headed down the hill.

'Does the bike have a pillion,' asked Caroline.

'It does,' replied Lance. 'But Raoul overlaps it a bit. I think the seating arrangements will bring tears to Ross's eyes.'

'I hope he knows what he's doing.'

They heard a distant back fire. They exchanged glances as each remembered the dreaded shot. But it wasn't they same sound.

As the morning air grew warmer and they felt they had lain long enough in the sun and all the interested or interesting parties seemed to be out of the resort they took a walk over to the point on the Villamaquis perimeter fence opposite where the trail of disturbed maquis had led Lance. It was not easy to establish the exact spot and Caroline suggested that Lance should repeat his walk and she would wait for him to appear on the opposite side. Lance was not at all keen on that plan. He liked to know exactly where Raoul was, preferably far away, when he went anywhere near the big man's usual beat.

So they continued their search trying to avoid making the sort of trampling themselves that they were looking for. The task was further confused by the casual track made by the security men just inside the perimeter. They were despairing of ever finding any clue when Caroline stopped to look at a brilliant cluster of bright red poppies in the midst of which grew a brazen yellow flower. It was as near a clash of colours as nature permits itself. Caroline recalled a piece of fabric Lance had brought her back from Copenhagen. She was about to draw Lance's attention to it, changed her mind and looked at it again. Now she saw that the poppies at one side of the clump which had looked as if they were past their best were in fact crushed; their leaves were flat on the ground. It was not on the security man's beat.

Lance look at the flowers, gave his wife a hug, then looked back to see if this were about the right place.

'Have you a thread or something. We can tie it on the fence and I can check from the other side when the coast is clear. Something inconspicuous.'

'Yes. I think I know where we can get just the thing.'

Her hand darted to his crotch and she pulled a thread from the inside leg of his shorts. 'This has been annoying me all day.'

'Easy does it, dear. You'll have me unravelled.'

'Relax. If tears had sprung to your eyes I would have known it wasn't a thread.'

She tied a tiny piece of the pale blue cotton to the mesh fence. 'It's this mystery I'd like to unravel. But we're maybe getting somewhere at last. You check the spot as soon as you dare then we can do a sweep from this side if we find this is the place.'

She looked at the mesh fence which was ten feet high but with no barbed wire or other deterrent on top. 'How on earth would anyone get a body over that?'

'How would you get a motor bike over a fence?'

The thread was in precisely the right place. Lance hurried back to tell Caroline, passing a worried looking Raoul on the way. Lance smiled and thought the big man would look even more worried if he knew what they had been up to.

They waited for siesta time, put on subdued clothes, took a small basket and made for the area they now knew must hold a clue for them. As they sauntered apparently aimlessly about Caroline picked some lavender, myrtle and other flowers she did not recognise and placed them in the basket in such a way that they were plainly visible to anyone they met. They walked a few paces apart and covered the ground in from the marked fence systematically.

From time to time they saw evidence of some compression of the grass and flowers but the helpfulness of this was diminished by the liberal attitude prevailing. There were no 'keep off the grass' signs or any other inhibitions on movement. In such a place flattened grass might have an innocent, well a fairly innocent, explanation. As the circle of their tracks widened they found they were coming close to one of the few old buildings in the compound. It was a square, squat building fashioned of large irregular stones in various shades of toffee. It had a neglected beauty. Apart from the flattened outward surface the stones had such a variety of rounded shapes that it seemed impossible that they should hold together, as they did, with no mortar or adhesive of any kind.

They decided a curiosity in such a building would be a perfectly natural reaction so they drew closer. The window openings were small and not glazed. The door was also small in proportion to the building. It was closed and looked to be of robust construction. They pushed but it did not yield. There was no one in sight so Lance heaved Caroline up so that she could peer through one of the high windows. When he lowered her to the ground she reported that the buildings seemed to have no internal walls and was empty except for some hay or straw in one corner. At one end there was a raised mezzanine type floor which she had not been able to see much of as it was dark and there seemed to be no sign of light fixtures.

'We may have to come back with a torch at night,' suggested Caroline.

'No,' objected Lance. 'Safer to use a torch in daylight.'

'True,' she agreed. 'We'll have to go back for that. I have a little one packed. If you brought it back from the crypt?' Lance nodded and Caroline continued. 'Before we go let's have a close look along the line between here and your pantie thread. This place seems so convenient for - .' She couldn't finish.

Caroline kept stooping to pick flowers and Lance conspicuously pointed out fresh colours which caught his eye meantime searching earnestly for any give away divergence from the random but recurring mixture of flower, stone and dust. She stopped by some fading white heather and was musing about how beautiful it must have been in the spring when she again noticed some flattened poppies. As she was beckoning Lance over she realised they were not poppies but small round splashes of dried blood.

CHAPTER THIRTEEN

Caroline was collating her lists of knowledge acquired so far when she stopped and sighed. 'We could have sent some of that blood to be checked if it had not already been done. I don't think there is any point in reporting it. Everyone seems preoccupied with a bigger it. I'll keep a note for later. I'm doing little drawings to remind us what happened here.' She looked at her list. 'There's a big gap here.'

Lance was looking over her shoulder earnestly trying to think of something useful to say. He was angry again. Having seen the blood he was desperate to contribute; to do something positive. But his mind was a blank. 'Many, I would say. Which one do you have in mind?'

'We have a nice pattern building up of movements during the day. But nothing of what happens at night after the revellers retire to their, or other's, various beds.'

Lance groaned in anticipation.

Part of the roof of each chalet was flat and was reached by a narrow external stair. There were two recliners and a small table with four white plastic coated chairs on each small elevated patio. Some residents lunched on their roof. Others no doubt sunbathed but, appropriately, they could not be seen when engaged in that activity. After dinner Lance and Caroline climbed up the stairs on their hands and knees and settled down with a piece of paper, a pencil, a pair of binoculars and a half bottle of duty free brandy.

As he sat there looking out into the darkness Lance was reminded of the old cemetery. The layout of the chalets was such that those higher up the hill looked down on all the others and over them to the bay beyond. Their chalet was only looked down on from the sisters' house and there was an impenetrable barrier of trees round that.

'I wish people would put out their lights before they do that.' remarked Caroline.

'Do what?' Lance seized the binoculars.

'Clean their teeth. I hate to see people cleaning their teeth. I was just testing to see if you were awake. It's one o'clock. Listen I'm going to stretch out on the recliner. Can you keep awake? Give me a shout in say, two hours.'

It was quiet. Sleepy quiet. Lance almost missed a group of naked figures making their way to the pool giggling conspiratorially. He heard quiet laughing and splashing. He felt awake again. He noted several movements included a late return of the Frenchman - alone. Then the bathers returned; one pair sharing a giant towel, the others flicking each others bare bodies with their towels and screaming with delight. Again Lance felt envious of their youth and of the time they lived in. He tried not to feel envious of their bodies.

The noise in the various chalets to which the bathers dispersed gradually faded away to nothing. Lance looked at his watch; he would give Caroline a little longer. She looked peaceful in the light of the thin sliver of moon which was rising from the distant water. He tucked her dressing gown around her affectionately.

They had never really been together like this for years. It was fun. Or it could have been. When the children were young he worked hard and saw little of them. He often, but not very often, thought that perhaps he had neglected her during this period. Caroline, unwilling to leave the children, had thrown herself into part time charity work. She had joined him in the firm when the girls were older. She was pleased she had. When the downturn came she was with him. When their own bankers had cooperated with the predator and coldly carved them up she was with him.

'You are too small to survive in this economic climate,' they had said and that was all the explanation or consultation he got. Caroline was there, tired, angry and bewildered with him. It was painful but a lot less painful than having to go home and explain to your wife such a disaster, such a failure. She knew and she understood.

He turned from her and tried to concentrate. It had been a long day and he had to fight to stay awake in the soft warmth of the night. His head dropped now and again but always the painful jerk woke him. He had just been thus roused when a light caught his eye. It shone from not far below him, as if a window had suddenly been illuminated. Been drinking too much, he thought, as he visualised someone struggling to find an unfamiliar toilet. Then the light went out. He turned away and only the corner of his eye detected that the light had gone on again. Then off - then on again - then off. It wasn't a window, too small and intense for that, and it did not seem to come from a chalet but somewhere half way between two of them.

A signal. Lance desperately looked around for an answering beam. He spun circling the darkness, round and round, then realising that two thirds of an arc would be all he had to cover if anyone was going to respond from where the light would have been visible. He concentrated on the mountain side. Then it came. High up in the hills a tiny speck of light flashed three times. The nearby light flashed again once.

Lance noted exactly where he stood and scratched a mark on the balustrade recording the direction of the hillside light. He tried to fix in his mind its height relative to the top of the black outline of the nearest tree. He then crept stealthily into the darkness in the direction the signal had come from. He tiptoed about for some time. He heard a variety of small sounds but saw no one.

In the morning they were able to pinpoint a little village high up the mountain which they had noticed previously twinkling in the evening blackness. They checked the name on their map - Olmacci. From the guide book they discovered that it had a population of two hundred and that there were small vineyards up there. The slope on which the village perched faced straight at the sun during the middle part of the day then deep shade slid over it as the sun moved across the sky. Some neighbouring slopes recessed far into the hillside never felt the warming rays - ever.

'You know the more I think about it the more I feel convinced that I've seen these signals before. Took them to be passing traffic. Headlights turning a corner or coming over bumps in the road. But I'm sure now that's what they were. Signals.'

They worked out that the signal from Villamaquis was not far from Jean Two's chalet; between that and another. They checked. The other chalet was that occupied by the Frenchman.

At breakfast Lance asked Donna about the little village now unseen but whose lights shone clearly high up the mountainside when the deep darkness of night descended on it. She confirmed that is was Olmacci, a small village without much to it but that approaching it you came to a beautiful stream which widened into tranquil pools as it run down over smooth stones. A favourite with sunbathers. She suggested they visit it. This idyllic spot was half a mile short of the village and a great place to spend a few hours, she advised.

Lance and Caroline decided they would go and have a look at this Olmacci in the quiet of the midday heat. In the meantime they reviewed their progress again.

'Possible clues so far. Shot – question mark. Stains in coffin. Various knick knacks from coffin. Signal from mountain village. Trampled grass by resting stones. Raoul's bike gets dumped near resting stones. Raoul's desire to kill some one. Blood by old storehouse. Signature in courtesy book.'

Lance looked over Caroline's shoulder as she methodically extracted from her long list those items she thought significant. 'Let's concentrate on the ones we can do something about.'

'Like breaking and entering the old storehouse?'

'Yes. And trying to get a sight of the stained courtesy book. And a visit to the mountain village.'

'Right, which one first?'

'Which two? Time is short now. Jean Two indicated something was happening soon - and our holiday is running out.'

'And no tan to take home. Questions will be asked. And innuendos will be directed at us.'

'Yes. Filthy swine. I only wish they were to be based on fact.' Lance smiled ruefully. 'But as I was saying let's go for two at a time. I reckon I can get into the storeroom with brute force and ignorance. Can you use your fragile charm to get at the book?'

'I can't think how but I'll try.'

Apart from the criss-crossing of the chalet girls there was very little activity mid morning so Lance prepared himself for his assault on the old stone building. He borrowed a clothes line from behind the chalets and wrenched a handle from a sweeping brush. He cut a shallow groove half way along the handle and tied the rope securely round the handle at that point.

He slung the rope in loops round his shoulder and held the broom handle like a scout pole. To a casual, short sighted and not too bright passerby he looked as if he were going to do some serious hill walking.

There was a choice of windows. The ones nearest ground level were securely boarded up. The two larger of the unboarded ones were also fairly near ground level but Lance spurned these as he wished his weight to be supported on the shortest possible section of the handle. The choice of a small window made the task of projecting the handle through a window much more difficult and his first few efforts just bounced off the wall. After a dozen attempts he sent the improvised spear through the square aperture but pulled on the rope too quickly and the whole device came back out. Another few attempts and it flew through again. This time he let the handle drop lower into the building, shook it about then pulled it back up slowly. He jumped up putting his weight on the rope and found that the handle was now wedged across the opening and the rope was dangling from almost the middle of it just as he had hoped.

As he started on the fourteen foot climb he noticed the handle bending under the weight. He patted himself on the back, but not literally, for choosing the small window; a longer stretch of handle would have snapped.

Using his feet to walk up the lower part of the wall he was soon within two metres of the window. He had to abandon the walk as the angle of the rope narrowed and change to pulling himself up bodily hand over fist the last part of the climb. He found this took all the strength he could muster. The rope was thin and did not provide a good grip. He brushed painfully against the rough wall as he ascended. The struggle became more difficult at the top as he could not just roll through the gap, the window was too small for that and the drop at the other side might be great enough to require that he land feet first.. He hoped earnestly that he would be over the mezzanine. He knew he couldn't be far from it.

He desperately tried to get his legs up to lead the way into the opening but could not do it. So he had no alternative but to squeeze through head first. He saw that he was over the raised section – just, and that there was a heap of hay just under him. Even at that he did not fancy landing on his head. Then he noticed just above the window the only beam in the building; obviously a support for the large shelf like structure below him. By excruciatingly painful contortions he reached up and got his arms round the old timber, swung in and let himself fall feet first into the hay just inches from the edge of the platform. He lay still for a long time as he regained his breath and rubbed his sore limbs.

He withdrew his climbing tackle from the window in case anyone passed and noticed it. Before moving further in he stopped and looked around to check a route which would cause the least disturbance to any possible helpful signs of previous activity. He looked closely at the straw he was lying on; almost half of the raised section was covered with the dried grasses. He could detect nothing out of the ordinary. As he stood up he could see with the help of a bright shaft of light from one of the windows that the other half had been swept clean. He moved to the edge of the shelf and, looking down, saw a round blackened area on the floor.

He stepped down a wobbling ladder. The last two rungs gave way under him and again he fell painfully. The rungs were charred. He examined the blackened floor. The whitewashed wall alongside was darkened. There was a smell of burning; a recent fire, thought Lance, but the charred traces were cold to his touch. He saw parts of old gardening tools, a steel bar bent double, metal rings with bolts which had obviously been attached to the wall a long time ago and some clay pots, mostly broken. He could find nothing helpful.

Directing his torch at the defiled patch he wondered what had been incinerated. He rejected the most gruesome possibility but as he turned away in disgust it occurred to him that if cremation had been the custom in these parts there would probably now be no body to search for.

'Bloodstained straw I would think. That's what they were burning,' guessed Caroline when they met.

While Lance had been at the old storeroom Caroline had set out a paper and pencil as she always did as an aid to orderly thought. She had looked at the pad, which was the one she normally used for her shopping list and for a moment wished she was engaged in just such a dull and routine task. But her excitement at the clues now presenting themselves mounted and quickly banished that thought from her mind. She listed possible plausible reasons she could give for wishing to see the soiled book. The list was short --

She thought Lance had been overcharged.

She wished to check on the name of a friend who had been here the previous week.

She was checking on her husband who was not allowed to drink whisky.

-- and unpromising.

Then came a flash of inspiration; not brilliant but better.

She hurried over to the courtesy bar before she lost her nerve. She looked carefully at the shelves of drinks as if making up her mind.
Shaking her head apparently undecided, hesitated, then walked over to the young lady at the desk.

'Excuse me. I had a lovely drink on my first day here. It was a mixture. Another guest - a young girl - bought it and shared it with me. It was delicious. I would love to have another.'

The girl looked up, puzzled. 'And how can I help?'

'The girl must have signed for it. Jean I think her name was. It was on our very first afternoon - Thursday. Not yesterday – the previous Thursday.'

'Yes?'

'The book has been changed. Sorry to be such a nuisance but I really liked that drink. It seemed to be the very flavour of the country. I felt I was tasting Corsica. Could we have a look and see what she signed for. If it's not too much bother.'

The girl's mouth said 'Nothing too much trouble for a guest.' But her eyes said. 'What sort of nut have I here?'

She was a long time in returning from the inner room already turning over the pages and muttering. 'Some idiot hid this away. Ah, here it is I think. Jean something . She has signed for an orange juice and a Campari. Together?'

Caroline peered at the entry which she could just read though it was upside down to her.

'That would be it. I tasted the orange but I didn't know what gave it the bite. I'll try one.'

She tried it and did not like it at all.

'So,' said Lance when they were exchanging reports. 'Let's assume that she drank the orange juice and her companion drank the Campari. I'll take a note of every one who has signed for Campari since. We're chasing a man or woman who drinks Campari. At last something to get our teeth into.'

CHAPTER FOURTEEN

The road to Olmacci was a cul de sac which meant that a drive up that route would look suspicious to any observer with reason to be wary of strangers. They decided to go to the pool Donna had told them about first; this would be a natural thing for tourists to do. They would sunbathe conspicuously then walk the last half mile as unobtrusively as they could and have a look at the village at close quarters.

As they had not been able to report the exchange of signals to Jean Two, who was becoming increasingly difficult to contact, they had decided that, whoever was doing the signalling, somewhere up there they might find a clue, or even a body. If it turned out to have been a signal from Jean, then they'd just have to be careful to avoid being a nuisance to her. So they set off in their new Volkswagen Polo. They appreciated its short wheel base as they navigated the sharp bends on the tortuous roads. As they started to climb the road sides were lined with Cypress Firs so they only had a good view over the bay when an area had been cleared for a vineyard. On these patches the symmetrically distorted looking bushes were heavy with grapes. They were almost at the pools when they first saw the Villamaquis far down below them.

'If we had powerful glasses we could lie up here and keep a check on all of them. There's no doubt someone down there knows what's going on.' Lance drew the car into a passing place and had a look through the binoculars at the sunbathers on some of the flat roofs but none of them were doing anything which would help them in their enquiries.

'They don't look as if they have anything to hide.'

From above the small white villas looked as if they had been designed not by an architect but by a confectioner.

'You can see the layout clearly. It has a pattern. The chalets are set like theatre seats so that each has a view between the others.'

'You've been to better theatres than I have. I wonder if anyone has been watching us - or Jean Two from up here.'

'I wonder.'

'They drove on to the pools. When they left the road and first saw the collection of blue pools on the white rock amongst the woods the area seemed completely deserted but as they scrambled down from the car they saw that the pools nearest the road each had a couple, partly dressed or completely undressed, enjoying the sun. They found a vacant pool further upstream and changed into to their swimsuits. The stone was piping hot underfoot. The water was clear and still. Even the small waterfalls flowed gently and quietly over the smooth stone. It was idyllic.

'Russell Flint,' said Lance looking around in admiration both at the scenery and at his wife stretched out in the sun. It occurred to him that Caroline would have looked well in a Russell Flint in something less efficiently concealing than the swimsuit. Caroline caught his look and smiled contentedly. After a time they emulated the fat little falls and slid quietly into the water. After the initial breathtaking shock they swam slowly and gracefully about the eccentrically shaped pool; it would have been sacrilegious to splash about in such serene surroundings. After a few very pleasant minutes they scrambled out and lay for some time looking up at the empty sky.

'This is being on holiday.' Caroline sighed and reached for Lance's hand.

'Perfect.'

In hats pulled well down, dark glasses and clothes they had not worn at Villamaquis before now, they walked up the steep road detouring into the woods whenever there was a path or anything which would seem reasonable to an observer that they should go to look at; just like interested tourists. Thus they visited small tinkling falls, patches of bright flowers and the occasional ruined cottage which even long past their useful lives were still beautiful as the sun illuminated the warm coloured stone. They enjoyed the walk and regretted arriving so soon at Olmacci. Their impatience for adventure had evaporated in the peaceful surroundings.

The village consisted of two rows of houses lined along either side of the road. The larger, finer houses faced over the valley and the bay. Those on the other side had a short view back into hills before the steep mountain soared into the sky.

A few huts stood dotted on fields behind the village but there was no sign of habitation further up the hillside.

Lance was adamant that the flashes had come from the village itself. They agreed if this were so they must have come from one of the houses facing the bay. There were eighteen of these.

There were no pavements but beaten paths on both sides of the road served as such and also as boundaries to the narrow strips of rough grass in front of each house. There were only a few cultivated gardens but masses of wild flowers filled the heavy, hot air with a strong perfume. Insects buzzed lazily. The houses faced onto the road with no fence but between each one there was a high barrier, sometimes topped with rusty barbed wire, linking the houses. It occurred to Lance that if anything unfortunate were to happen there was nowhere for them to go or hide. There were no men about. No doubt, he thought, all out in the vineyards. A few women were working in the gardens but most sat in the shade of their doorways apparently sewing or lace making.

A small display of fruit and vegetables projected from one doorway and Caroline, affecting a broad American accent, stopped and bought some grapes.

The village ended abruptly as if no-one would build a house outside the protection of close neighbours. They decided to try to have a look at the other side of the houses but the ground fell steeply away on that side making this difficult. They did try by scrambling down the slope, selecting a spot with lots of cover and turned to have a look up at the village from there.   All of the houses had large fences at the back. They could see only the upper halves of the uniformly two storied buildings and saw that, unlike the seaside houses there were no flat roofs; too much rain up here they thought. They noted that several houses had barred windows whereas others had verandahs with the windows left open.

Apart from that, nothing made one house stand out from the others. No extensions, no porches, no dormer windows, no changes since they were built.

Discouraged they lay down and ate some grapes; they were delicious.

'I feel flat and drained,' said Caroline.   'Thank goodness it's downhill to the car.'

'I wish it were uphill. Then we could look down on this blasted place.' Lance's eyes searched around then widened. 'Look. As it goes up out of the village the road bears right – see over there. From here it looks as if the hill rises very steeply from the road beyond that point. If we could get a little way up that slope we might see along the back of the houses. There might be something in the back gardens which would give us a clue.'

'Steeply you said,' complained Caroline half an hour later looking up at the precipitous crags rearing from the edge of the road now turned rough track. It looked impossible for any other than a skilled rock climber to get even a short way up. Again they felt discouraged. The heat multiplied the difficulty of every move.

'Do you remember what Kirsty said?'

'No, I don't.' Caroline was short.

'She said, find a stream and it leads you to heaven.'

Caroline nodded unenthusiastically and they walked on. They had covered half a mile before they came to a stream of water falling a vertical ten feet before disappearing under the road. Caroline looked dismayed.

'We were never told that the road to heaven was an easy one.' Lance looked around for a foothold.

'Let's see if we can find the primrose path.'

'Shame on you, lass. That leads to the bad place.'

'So what's different?'

Lance found a part of the cliff which had several strong bushes growing from crevasses.

'If we get up this first rock face I think it's bound to ease up a bit. We can't see the upper slopes so it must slope back. Let me blaze a trail.'

He gripped a bush about five feet from the ground and pulled himself up. He was now within three feet of another. That was easy.

The next one gave under him - Caroline gasped - but his foot slid back to a narrow projection on the rock face. Thus he proceeded slowly and, with a struggle, he got to the top and disappeared from sight.

He lay down and poked his head over the edge then, puffing heavily he gasped. 'Would you rather I did this and you just wait for me here?'

'No thanks. I'm not waiting here on my own.'

'But do you have the strength to get up here?'

'Not to carry an overweight body like that but I think I could just about manage this sylph like figure.'

'Good girl. Let's be having you then. Careful now.'

Caroline had to use hands, elbows, feet and knees to make the top, skinning elbows and knees on the sharp rock and tearing her hands on the jagged bushes.

'I'm daft. I should have waited for you. I hope we're not going down that way.'

'We'll find an easier descent I'm sure.'

As Caroline bent to take a thorn out of her knee Lance gasped. 'You've hurt yourself. Look.' He pointed to a large purple stain spreading on the side of her shorts. He rolled over to her side and held her hand. 'Oh, Caroline. You've lost a lot of---,'

Caroline turned, alarmed, looked down, felt the discoloured area and laughed. 'Grapes. That's the last gone I'm afraid. It's all right. I'll buy some more.'

Lance laughed to hide his intense relief.

They were now standing on a shelf about twenty feet across alongside a calm pool which held the water awaiting its descent over the fall; the clear liquid then folded itself gently over the edge. As they turned towards the village the ground sloped upwards giving promise of a good view point but also indicating that the cliff between them and the road grew higher the nearer they got to their objective. They headed that way keeping as far as they could from the precipice. After about four hundred yards the whole hillside swept to the right and soon they could see the village.

To get a good view they had to go nearer the edge than they would have wished. There was some surreptitious jockeying for position.

Gripping the strongest supports available, rough, stunted mountain trees, they looked back at the village and Lance directed their binoculars down the valley. They were about a hundred feet higher than the houses and could see along the back gardens not visible from the road or the lower hillside. Mostly they were neatly sown with vegetables but two were completely neglected; all the houses had appeared occupied when they walked past.

Lance focussed his binoculars on the two unkempt houses Nothing moved. In the nearest of the two an old greenhouse looked as if it were still in use. Throughout the entire village only two Van Gogh like figures could be seen; women bent over their vegetable patches.

Caroline washed her scrapes and scratches in a trickle of clear water which tumbled past. They took turns in watching while the other stretched cramped legs. A donkey stirred and walked freely up the village street. A feather of smoke rose slowly from a chimney.

Lance ducked his head down behind a bush. 'Get down, Caroline. Someone in that faraway house has his binoculars pointed at our binoculars.'

Lance rolled quickly for a few yards as if it were a sniper observing them and urgently signalled Caroline to do the same. They lay still, heads close to the ground for a short time then raised their eyes cautiously from their new position. They heard a distant clip clop as the donkey broke into a gallop. It was quiet again. Then moments later three people dashed out from the house they had been watching and rushed down the road, which they could see between the houses, zig zagging from side to side, causing the donkey to about turn and break into an ungainly gallop. The group of runners disappeared from their sight behind an ancient hut. Within seconds a car roared from that direction on to the road and sped downhill towards the coast. Lance had the glasses on the car. Caroline nudged him and pointed back towards the house.

As he turned a muffled roar and a shock wave reached them. The walls of one of the houses swung slowly outwards like a cardboard box being unfolded then it disappeared in a great ball of dust.

One woman appeared at the front of almost every house and looked towards the stricken dwelling. Slowly they congregated, those nearest the explosion walking backwards to miss nothing. Pieces of wood and stone now flew upwards out of the dust and fell all over the village causing the women to abandon their curiosity and rush into one of the other houses for shelter from the deadly rain. A few moments later a young boy raced from the refuge and sped up the hill. As the thick cloud settled flames could now be seen and smoke mingled with the dust. Lance and Caroline could smell the fumes even from where they were.

'What do you make of that?' croaked Caroline.

'I'm sure one of the three runners was Jean Two.' Lance turned the binoculars down the road but the car was now well out of sight.

'Well, thank heavens she got away in time. And good to see that she had some others with her.'

'With one killed already they were bound to try to protect her. I hope they will guard her from now on. And she will have to be less conspicuous.'

'Might be difficult to do whatever she's doing without being visible. But perhaps one of these other two can take it on now. I hope so.'

'They looked a burly pair of lads.'

'Do you think there's anyone left in there? No-one seems to be going to find out.'

'I think the wee lad will be away to get the men.'

The donkey was now returning down the road completely bewildered but again stopped, sniffed the air and relieved itself energetically.

'I wish it wouldn't do that,' mumbled Lance.

It now turned back up the road at a shambling gallop.

Lance turned the glasses on the road at the point where the donkey had been startled. He looked carefully then croaked. 'That branch. Look, in the middle of the road. That burnt branch has fingers – five fingers.'

Caroline took the binoculars and stared wide eyed at the gruesome fragment. 'Look Lance. The fingers are twitching.' She turned away feeling sick.

'You would be twitching too if you were as hot as that.'

Lance tried to sound matter of fact.

Caroline's face was pale but her voice was steady. 'Someone should get there quickly. Someone else in there may be hurt. Or anywhere in the village with all that flying glass. We'll have to go down, Lance.'

'Sure. Did you see Paul Newman and Robert Redford jump off the cliff in 'The Sundance Kid'?' Caroline nodded. 'Well, it would be just like that except no water at the bottom.'

Caroline peered over the edge and quivered. 'I hope we can find a sensible way down or you can go and bring a helicopter.'

As they moved more quickly now along the ridge towards the village they saw the first of the men appear hurrying down from the vineyards, backs still bent from the day's toil.

Lance slowed down a little and nodded towards them. 'They will contact the police. We can safely leave it to them now.'

'I like the safely.' Caroline responded nodding vigorously. She was thoughtful as they struggled along the hillside. 'You know, I don't believe much in coincidences. I think our binoculars triggered off that evacuation. Somebody thought we were somebody else.'

'I think you are something else, darling. Let's see. You said there were binoculars pointing at our binoculars then everyone came out before the big bang. At least almost everyone. Something made them panic – and I think you're right. It was us. Lucky they weren't all killed. That was a serious explosion.'

'So, if some of them got clear our day has not been in vain.' He paused. 'I hope Jean One's body was not in there or--' He shrugged and looked miserable, '-or what? Look let's stay up here till we're past the village and get as near to the car as possible before we go down. If we're seen our presence may be misunderstood.'

'Or worse still – understood.'

They clambered slowly and painfully along the ridge which varied from a narrow slope to vertiginous ledge. They heard the sound of fire and/or police vehicles coming up the hill.

'Good. We won't need to jump now,' gasped Caroline.

CHAPTER FIFTEEN

There was no sign of Jean Two when Lance and Caroline eventually arrived back at Villamaquis tired and anxious. They had taken time to have a quick swim when they reached the mountain pool scratched and leg weary after a difficult detour along the hillside necessitated by their desire to stay out of sight of anyone in Olmacci. They had excused to themselves this indulgence amidst the distress by agreeing that they would have to clean up anyway before approaching Villamaquis but, although they did not admit it to each other, they badly needed the break after the shock of the afternoon's events. Caroline noted sadly that there was nothing boyish about Lance's face now.

Jean Two did not appear for dinner. No-one remarked on this as she had become irregular in her appearances nor, as she did not contribute much to the jollity or interest of the meal times, was she really missed; only the Lockharts gave much thought to her. The talk was mainly of the feast of St Erasmus, patron saint of seafarers which was to take place that Saturday. Donna described it as a seaside Henley Regatta. It was evidently a big event, the highlight of the village year. No one mentioned the incident of the exploding house. Obviously the news had not yet reached Villamaquis; if it ever would. Lance and Caroline did not raise the subject.

When they retired to bed that night Caroline reminded Lance that he had said that any smugglers were at their most vulnerable at the coast and at airports.

'I'm sure that's so,' said Lance, 'why?'

'Well, if I were going to do something nefarious by the seashore I would do it when there is a lot of other activity, like when every one was celebrating the sailor's saint. Wouldn't you?'

'You're a genius. Of course I would. They said a police boat won something last year so it sounds as if even they will have other things on their mind. I wonder if Jean Two has thought of that. I wish we could contact her.'

'After today's incident she'll be lying low. There's no point in discussing this afternoon's events with her. She knows all about that and would definitely not be pleased to know that we were onlookers. If our binoculars saved her life, great, but we'll have to forego the thanks. So the two of us will have to watch Brodie, the Frenchman and Raoul. Let's go to sleep and see if the subconscious comes up with anything.'

The exhausted Lance acquiesced to that.

They lay in bed turning the day's activities over in their minds but not talking, Lance lying with his arm round Caroline, too tired to do other than give an occasional affectionate squeeze, then suddenly he sat up violently pulling the corner of the sheet towards him.

'What's that?'

Caroline peered with sleepy eyes at the cloth in Lance's hand. 'A laundry mark. What do you expect – a coat of arms? Listen it's warm but I don't even like a warm draught. Let go of that sheet.'

Lance went quiet and kept looking at the mark.

'Well?'

'I'm thinking.'

'It's past thinking time. Let go.'

'Caroline. I've seen this mark before.'

'In this bed I hope.'

Lance gulped. 'In the coffin – Fournier's coffin. The shroud had a mark like that.'

'Do shrouds have a laundry mark?' asked Caroline half mocking.

'Surely not.'

'So?'

Lance passed the corner of the sheet to Caroline. 'So Monsieur Fournier was wrapped in a bed sheet – perhaps from here.'

'Because his original shroud had marks of --' Her voice broke, ' - poor Jean.'

Lance put his arms round her again. 'Looks like it. Remember I told you about Donna getting a bollocking from Mona for losing a sheet.'

'So, this clinches it. There was an extra body in the coffin for a time. Long enough to move it from somewhere to the crypt. And long enough for it to stain Fournier's shroud.'

'Then it was moved again after that half face saw you when you went to the grave for the first time so it wasn't there when I paid my visit. Must have thought you were on to him and he had to move it quickly.'

'Never mind the first – the only time. So, her body was there when I was in the crypt.'

Lance tried to sound business like. 'Well, this certainly reinforces some of our suspicions but I don't know if it gets us much further forward.'

'Except that it confirms that some one from here is involved. And whoever it is might be gone by the time an enquiry starts about poor Jean. Guests are departing all the time. So, it really is a job for us – us. Only we can find out the truth in time. We are the only ones who seem to be even trying. And we're on the right trail. The person we are looking for is here on our doorstep. We can concentrate our efforts now.'

'Right, a good night's sleep then let's go for it.'

Caroline lay for a long time thinking about how near she had been to the body.

Next morning there was a thin film of cloud misting the sky so they felt a little more energetic. At breakfast the Brodies spoke enthusiastically of a visit they had made the previous day to Ajaccio to see where Napoleon was born. Lance almost quipped that this was change of interest for them but bit back the words.

'Was he buried in Corsica?' he asked.

'No,' replied Brodie. 'He was interred in Paris. Hotel des Invalides.'

'Funny place for a corpse - a hotel. A long term guest I suppose,' interjected Ian.

'It's not a hotel in that sense.' There was no hint of humour in Brodie's voice. 'We stayed at the Marriott when we were in Paris. Magnificent hotel. The best.' Mabel's eyes dipped and her shoulders twitched.

When the Brodies left Caroline remarked that Albert wore no rings although Mabel was festooned with them. 'I remember reading once that criminals and people who don't want to be remembered don't wear rings.'

'Sounds logical. But it sometimes reflects the work they have to do.'

'What work?'

'I don't want even to think about it.'

'He has cold eyes. Not exactly cruel. Cold. Dispassionate.'

In his now routine check at the courtesy bar Lance noticed that two guests had ordered Campari. Both were outwith their present list of suspects and after tracing them he found that one was a young lady, brown all over who spent all her time by the pool as near naked as made very little difference. The other was the male half of a couple who had arrived just three days ago. They were 'eliminated from their enquiries'.

Lance was standing outside the bar with two unwanted orange juices in his hand when he noticed the bus driver coming towards the offices as usual at this time. Again, as always, with the brief case in his hand. Suddenly he drew back off the path. Looking around to see if there was any apparent reason for this strange behaviour Lance saw Raoul striding towards them. Lance's first instinct was to duck out of sight also but it was too late. Raoul hurried towards him and he braced himself but with a polite 'excusez moi' the big man brushed past him. Lance noticed that the bus driver held up his case as Raoul came past him as if to hit the big man if he were threatened. Raoul passed with a glower. The bus driver scampered off.

Lance stood still and could hear the two sisters talking loudly in obvious disagreement. Mona sounded angry and aggressive whereas Rhoda sounded conciliatory. Raoul only interjected occasionally and briefly. As the voices stopped Lance moved away just in time to avoid a distressed looking Raoul charging out of the door. He turned and looked back flexing his great fists then shook his head and departed. The sound of the bike exploded angrily as if he had given it a harder kick than usual.

Lance stretched himself out by the pool having selected a recliner facing the office. The sky was now clearer and the temperature rising. He beckoned Caroline over to tell her of the fracas. Shortly afterwards Rhoda hurried out holding a handkerchief to her face. She headed towards the bungalow.

'Well, is that a business tiff, a love affair gone sour or something relevant to our case?'

'Search me,' responded Caroline.

'With pleasure.'

'Hands off, you fool. We must get to know more of the sisters. That's the only way we're going to find out what Raoul is up to.'

'Well, we heard that the one function they always attend is the grand buffet. Which is tonight. It is also the only occasion when we don't stick with our own dining group. We might be able to get close to one or both of them.'

'If we get a choice let's have Rhoda. Mona is a bit fierce for me.'

'And Rhoda seems to have some sort of relationship with Raoul which it would be helpful to know more about. I wonder if he will be there. If so, don't let's sit next to him. He is intimidating to put it mildly. He certainly puts the frighteners on the bus driver. You should have seen him cower? Talking of whom did you notice he came out with a package in his hand.'

'The takings for the bank. Like I said.'

'Probably, but why does he not put them in the brief case?'

'Yes, that is strange. I can't think why. Another mystery to solve.'

'Do you notice that Raoul can't keep his eyes off the case.'

'What's in it I wonder?'

CHAPTER SIXTEEN

Caroline offered to make up a picnic for the middle of the day but said she wanted to have a lie in the sun before they set off. Lance opted to go for a stroll, impatient to make more contact with the possible suspects and get closer to them. The first contact happened sooner than he planned. He saw the Brodies turn a corner ahead of him. As a matter of, what had become, routine he turned after them. To his surprise, after a short distance, Albert Brodie stopped and, as Lance hesitated, the thin man turned and faced him with a set grim expression on his face. He looked angry but embarrassed and nervous. Lance tried to step around him but Brodie performed a neat chasse and blocked his way.

'You have been following us,' he challenged.

Lance could think of nothing to say.

'What are you after? Is it Mabel?'

Lance looked at Mrs Brodie and politely restrained a smile.

'You have a lovely wife of your own. Why don't you behave yourself like grown man? If you do not, I will go to Caroline and tell her what you are up to and if that doesn't put an end to it then, big man as you are, I'll – I'll punch your nose.' He quivered with indignation.

Lance searched for a reply in a totally confused mind.

'No, you have got this all wrong Mr Brodie. I can explain.'

'Go on then, explain.'

'It is difficult. This is confidential. I don't want it to be known what I am doing.'

'I am sure you don't.' The tall man drew back his thin arm and swung it at Lance who easily blocked the feeble blow.

Lance decided that he would have to tell something like the truth. He obviously couldn't go on watching the man now whatever the outcome of this encounter. He sounded genuinely upset but Lance was wary that it could be a bluff. If that were the case perhaps he could try a bluff too and trick Brodie into giving away what he knew. As Caroline had said, he wasn't the type to be a big cog.

Lance set his face as solemnly as he could in the ridiculous position in which he found himself. 'A serious crime has been committed and your interest in graves has been noted and has aroused suspicion so I have been instructed to keep an eye on you. What we have to find out is - and I have other ways of finding out if you do not cooperate – are you involved in the crime or are you just an innocent ghoul?' Lance scowled in what he hoped was an intimidating manner.

The now nervous looking couple started to speak hurriedly.

'Crime?' squeaked Albert.

'What are you talking about? Ghoul. Albert is an undertaker,' protested Mabel.

'A mortician,' interrupted Albert.

'A good one. He has built up a wonderful little business.'

'Not so little, darling.'

'He is going to write a book, "The World of Burials" he is going to call it, or "The Mortician Through The Ages."

Lance glowered and looked disbelieving as she hesitated and then, desperate to dispel any suspicions her words poured out.

'Everywhere we go he researches. Every where. We take holidays where there are interesting graves, burial places or customs. I see more funeral parlours than ice cream parlours, more gravesides than seasides.' She spoke eloquently as if she was bursting to express her feelings, using phrases she had pent up for years. 'I get sick of it I can tell you. But he is an enthusiast. And a man must have an enthusiasm, must he not? And, as you can see he does very well.' Her voice tapered off.

'And I am going to do better. They are away ahead of us in the States. I want to adopt some of their methods. Improve on them even. Package funerals. Prepaid preferably. A real all in comprehensive service. Easier for the client and more profitable for the undertaker. From cradle to the grave was always an idle dream, but from death to the grave should not be impossible.'

Lance, now completely bemused, decided to let them talk on until he could get his bearings again.

'Personalised hymns. Some are easy to adapt. Upwards Peter Rodgers goes just as well as Onward Christian Soldiers. Some would be more difficult. Need to employ some one.'

'Like the ones who write the messages on birthday cards,' suggested Lance.

Albert frowned, but would not be deflected. 'A far greater choice of coffin, both in materials and colour. Green coffins for those against wasting good timber; breaks my heart when I see good mahogany or oak going up in smoke.' Lance nodded appreciatively at this last remark.

Albert continued. 'A more appropriate range of flowers could be cultivated. A really memorable Garden of Remembrance. Much more imaginative monuments. I would employ a real sculptor. Photographs, suitably protected, at the graveside as they have in many countries.'

'Death masks,' suggested Lance sarcastically.

'Now there's a thought,' agreed Albert seriously. 'And perhaps, if local bye-laws will allow, funeral pyres for the ethnic minorities who wish to depart the world that way. Or Viking type boats sailing off over the horizon.'

'We live by the canal, Albert,' interrupted Mabel.

'The urn has long been considered the receptacle for the respectable. That sounds good doesn't it? You have got to learn to turn a phrase in marketing, Mister Lockhart. And there must be a market for greater choice. You know – a hollowed out cricket ball for a cricketer for example. A plant pot for a gardener. The possibilities are endless.'

'I'm sure,' mumbled Lance trying to keep the sarcasm out of his voice.

'Ministers and Priests are too conservative. I had the recorded voice of the deceased joining in on a duet with his brother at one funeral. The voice coming from the direction of the casket. That took some timing. It brought a tear to the eye.'

'It would have brought tears to both of mine.' Lance shook his head.

'But the priest didn't like it.'

'And my part.' interjected Mabel, 'Mail order. The recently bereaved don't know what they want or what is available. I would sell our mailing list. A service to solicitors, estate agents, printers, caterers, drapers – mourning clothes you know, sellers of burglar alarms.' She paused for breath then after a moments hesitation went on. 'Even, perhaps spiritualists and, after a decent interval, dating agencies.'

Lance opened his mouth to protest but Albert started on his diatribe again. 'Embalming, mummifying. Mortal remains leave evidence of our history to those coming after. They can't lie like history books. We are leaving nothing these days, nothing.'

Albert voice began to rise and Mabel's shoulders to twitch.

'Right, Albert. We get the idea. Don't we Mister Lockhart?'

'Absolutely,' agreed Lance. 'Oh, absolutely.'

'I am going to learn everything about the trade – profession. Everything. And I will go anywhere, every where. There is so much to learn.'

Albert was getting his second wind so Lance decided to seize the initiative. 'I now understand your interest. But why did you go to Monsieur Fournier's crypt? Why that one? What was so special about it? Hundreds like it surely.'

'Oh no. Not so. I was in Monsieur Duval's funeral parlour – primitive affair – when I heard him discuss with one of his staff an order for a special custom built coffin. Monsieur Duval did not want to discuss it with me. Anxious he looked, when I asked him about it. Worried. Trade secret perhaps. So I went up to look for myself. Curiosity, that's all.'

'Research, Albert,' supported Mabel.

'And did you find out what was different?'

'Oh yes. The coffin could be opened just by tugging the lid upward. I noticed the join on the side. I tried it. It came away with about three inches of the coffin sides and ends. There was a fillet attached to the lower part of the casing, projecting upwards, so it was a tight enough fit. Wouldn't just pop open while it was being carried. But you could open it quite easily if you knew what to do.'

'Easy,' thought Lance flexing his still sore fingers. 'Would that be why it was solid oak?'

'Probably. So you know about coffins too, Mister Lockhart.'

'No. Furniture. But the same thing basically.'

Lance recalled the unnecessary long agonising minutes unscrewing the lid. And it could have been so simple. He thought of a second body being dumped in the coffin at the resting stones. That now seemed much more plausible.

'Why do you think they did that?'

'I haven't been able to work that out. I visited Ravel's parlour again and talked around it but he was giving nothing away. I'll give it some more thought.'

'But why did you go back to the crypt again?'

'How do you know about that? Was that you at the crypt?' Albert's eyes widened.

Lance nodded.

'You frightened the life out of me. I went back because I was sure I saw blood on the first visit. Didn't occur to me at the time but of course there should not have been blood. Not after the body had been - processed. I should have thought of that then but I was - .' He stopped himself confessing any unprofessional weakness. 'Did you see? Was there blood?' he asked Lance.

'No. All wiped away - I think. Perhaps it was wine - red wine. Perhaps it just evaporated.'

'I know blood when I see it. Seen enough of it. I think I should report this to the local police.'

Lance thought of discouraging this idea but could think of no way of doing so without getting deeper into the mire so he tried to side track his man. 'Mister Brodie, let me ask you. Did you see if the shroud was marked - or anything unusual in the coffin?'

'Oh, I didn't look inside. Oh no. I can tell you it wasn't empty if that's what in your mind. If it had been the coffin would have lifted when I pulled up the lid. No, it felt quite heavy. But I wouldn't look in. Got to show respect. In this business - got to show respect. No point pretending. People see through that. The bereaved is in a very sensitive frame of mind.' He had that unctuous look on his face that would have made the average mourner cringe 'See through any sham. Hurts them.' Then more briskly. 'Won't bring you any more business!'

'Well. Well. Sorry to have troubled you. But you will understand my dilemma. I have never heard you talk of your – profession.'

'I was telling Kirsty all about it yesterday.'

'At length,' interjected Mabel.

Ignoring her Albert continued, 'A pity you weren't there then we would not have had this misunderstanding.'

Mabel now asked pointedly what his interest in the crypt had been. Lance flashed a credit card at them and tapped the side of his nose. 'I promise you as soon as this is cleared up you will be the first to know.'

Lance looked at his watch, feigned alarm and excused himself and rushed off on the pretext of meeting Caroline. Just before he hurried away Brodie pressed a business card into his hand as if to confirm his story. Lance kept rushing until he was out of sight then relaxed as he realised he didn't know where he was going or where he wanted to go. As he slowed down he fumed about the hours, days of wasted time and the dull, dull journeys.

Lance was angry when he arrived back at the villas after wandering aimlessly about for a long time. He had not been too unhappy to give up the usual pleasures of a holiday when he thought he was serving a purpose; a noble purpose. Now he felt like a prize idiot. He punched his hand and wished he had something or somebody to punch. He would normally have looked forward to seeing Caroline and making a great joke of the Brodies disclosures with a stream of merry quips but he was not in that mood. He was glad Caroline was not with him.

As he was nearing their chalet he saw Ross and his eyes lit up.

As Lance braced himself to intercept him he almost gloated as he anticipated that the young man might be at his weakest right now, returning to his own chalet from the direction of Donna's. But not for the first time since he arrived in Corsica he hated what he was stiffening his resolve to do. He liked Ross and even more so he liked Donna. At the moment he was not sure he liked himself. Only his present evil temper and his determination to get at the killer of the beautiful Jean allowed him to descend to this depth.'

'Can I have a word with you, Ross?'

'Sure, Lance. What can I do for you?'

'I am interested to know what you do for Raoul? That man intrigues me.'

'Yes. He's quite a man. But sorry, confidential. That's part of the deal.'

'I won't breathe a word.'

'No chance. Firstly – I have given my word and secondly and marginally more important, Raoul would break my neck. Look, I want to get to my b—chalet. Do you mind?'

Ross made to pass but Lance blocked his way.

'Look, Lance don't get heavy with me or I might get my big friend to have a word with you. I hear he had a dust up with a local who thought he was a hard man three weeks ago. They're still trying to reassemble him up at the hospital.'

'I'm sure you're right, and I hate to do this, Ross but before I start let me say this – believe it or not – I need this information for a good cause.'

'Not as good a cause as keeping my neck intact. Now please. I'm tired and you are beginning to get on my wick.'

Lance took a deep breath. 'Donna would be sacked if the sisters heard of your – involvement. It is strictly against the rules.'

'You bastard.'

'Not really. Good cause. I told you. Also important, serious and urgent. I must know.' He paused. 'She likes her job.'

'Blackmail. I'll tell the police.'

Again Lance breathed hard, then growled. 'Go on then. Tell me.'
Ross's face slackened. He looked bewildered and defeated.

'Look, I wouldn't do anything to hurt that girl. She is a little sweety. We haven't been doing anyone any harm. Back off will you?'

'Don't misunderstand me. The only feelings I have about you and Donna is of extreme jealousy. I also have a high regard for her. But I must know. That overrides all other considerations with me at this time.'

Lance looked mean but had to struggle to keep a sympathetic look off his face. Ross's head dropped and he thought for a moment, then shrugged.

'I follow the bus driver. Find out where he goes each day. Three days I've done this. Tomorrow will be the last.'

'And where does he go?'

'He goes to the airport every second day but you will know that. He drives the Villamaquis bus when the other driver is not available.'

'Who does he talk too? What does he do?'

'He drives the bus.' Ross managed a tone of defiance then changed his mind when Lance scowled. 'He always talks to the café owner on his way back from the airport. He always reports to the sisters on his return. He always carries a brief case with him. For carrying his rake off for providing a bus load of customers to the café, I've no doubt. His services seem to be appreciated there. He goes to the bank. Look, if Raoul is going to jump him for the cash, I'm not involved – and I don't want to be.'

'I'll keep you out of this. I promise. Go on.'

'He went up the mountain road this morning – the one to Olmacci but he took the left fork after a mile. It goes over open ground up there so I didn't dare follow him further. Raoul was insistent that I shouldn't be rumbled. No chances, he said. He seemed interested in that trip. There's not much else. The driver is obviously afraid of Raoul and avoids him. He lives in the village. In some sort of digs. He drinks in the scruffy little pub by this end of the harbour. The sign is broken and dilapidated. So I don't know what it is called. I only stayed in a minute. Looks like a scene from Treasure Island. You know the sort where they press ganged crews for His Majesty's navy in ye olden days. Every eye turned on me and I would have beaten a hasty retreat but I'd already bounced back off the pong. He keeps bad company does Bernard.'

'Bernard is it? Bernard the bus driver. Sounds like a character from Thomas the Tank Engine.'

Ross half smiled. 'I can't make him out. Even when he's saying something pleasant that dustpan brush moustache of his keeps you from knowing whether he is smiling or not.'

'Thanks, Ross. I'm really sorry to have put the screws on you. What you do is none of my business. You've been very helpful. Thank you. You can rely on me. Neither Raoul or the sisters will hear a word of this – chat. I am most grateful.'

'Can I go now?'

Lance nodded and Ross turned on his heels and hurried off.

Lance was not in good form when they settled in their picnic spot. They looked down on a small deserted, sandy bay flanked by rugged sand coloured rocks. The water was calm and sapphire clear. They lay among the flowers with their backs on warm smooth stones. There whole world looked beautiful. But Lance looked unhappy. Caroline looked at a face which showed its age – and more. Not since back when the business was folding had she seen him look like this. She tried to flatter and flirt him out of the mood. It invariably worked, but this time he did not respond.

He was still beset by a mood of self loathing.

Caroline abandoned her amorous efforts and served a glass of cool wine then, in tune with his frame of mind, asked him how he had got on this morning. Lance was silent and Caroline waited. In his own time he started. He decide to speak first of his encounter with Ross and get that off his chest. It was only when Caroline expressed great enthusiasm for the information he had obtained that he brightened up.

He then told her of his meeting with the Brodies. She was soon rolling on the ground with laughter.

'I have heard of life imitating art but not death.'

Lance now laughed. The boyish look returned.

'Tailor made coffins. I like that. I believe they do that in Ghana. And what customized casket do you wish, Lance? Ashes would fall through a lady's garter. I think a commode. In honour of your years of devotion to the furniture industry. An unused one of course.'

'No. I think a Sancerre bottle – half filled. Then I could soak away through all eternity.'

'Well, that would give you continuity. I think a collecting box would best reflect my efforts in this life. I always seem to have a collecting box in my hands.

You would see that the slot was sealed wouldn't you, dear. And don't put a single penny in. I don't want to go on being rattled after I have cast off my mortal whatsit.'

When the frivolity wore thin they returned to the serious matter of the information gleaned from Ross. It was agreed that Lance should go alone the next day, immediately after breakfast, to see what lay up the track taken by the bus driver. If the vicious looking Raoul was interested in what the nasty looking Bernard was doing up there, it must be of interest to them.

If their conflict was coming to a head it must surely be relevant to their quest.

CHAPTER SEVENTEEN

Lance was relieved that this was buffet night so that he would not have to sit at the same table as Ross. Raoul was present but he did not join in the party or eat with them but hovered over the revellers watching everyone but also looking outwards from time to time.

'He's on guard,' whispered Caroline.

'Guarding who from what?'

'I'll ask Rhoda.'

By dint of some skilful and ruthless, not to say rude, manoeuvring they managed to get a couple of seats near to Rhoda. She was being charming and outgoing to those seated beside her most of whom were trying to get information from her or taking the opportunity to voice tiny complaints or suggestions. Rhoda fielded them all expertly and with good grace promising immediate action when it seemed appropriate. They could see that she positively bristled with pride in their happy establishment.

Lance noticed that her cheek was grazed and whispered to Caroline. 'Someone has hit her.' Caroline nodded.

'Are there quarries up in those hills?' asked Lance gesturing in the direction of Olmacci.

'No. I don't think so. Why?' Rhoda looked puzzled.

'I saw a great plume of smoke yesterday afternoon. An explosion of some sort, I would think.'

Someone interjected to say that she had also seen a great cloud of smoke and heard a loud rumble which she had thought was thunder.

'Bandits,' someone else suggested, before Rhoda could reply.

'I don't think it could have been either a quarry or bandits but I will let you know if I hear anything.' She said this with the air of someone who had no such intention.

Later they saw her whispering to a grim faced Raoul.

The spread of colour coordinated salads, the array of cold meats and fish, the barbeque smells, the artistically stacked fruit and the copious quantity of wine made it difficult for the Lockharts to concentrate on the subtleties of the exchanges going on around them. Jean Two sat at Mona's table but seemed to be giving the food her undivided attention. Unusually she was dressed elegantly.

Caroline nodded over towards her. 'I was going to say she is dressed to kill, but I won't. Very impressive. These shoes alone would take a month's wages.'

'Daddy no doubt,' averred Lance. 'She wants to look as if she is on holiday.'

At that table Mona was holding forth in the same friendly manner as Rhoda. Christophe was in earnest conversation with a shapely blond and was oblivious to all else.

'Why,' asked Caroline, 'do I always think of Prince Charming when I look at him?'

'Not me. I think of Maurice Chevalier and his Thank Heaven for Little Girls. Anyway don't you be trying to see if the glass slipper or anything else fits.'

'Ah jealous. I like that in a man.'

They rose and circulated with glasses in their hands. The hubbub of conversation was rising by the minute and evidence was increasing that a great deal of alcohol had been drunk. Couples were heading for the pool noisily and couples were heading for the chalets quietly. There was no riotous behaviour. Lance came face to face with the probable reason for this, Raoul, and thinking he must get to know all the players in this grim game he swallowed hard and spoke to him.

'You are a good shot, Monsieur.'

The large man, obviously uncomfortable in a casual suit, looked carefully at Lance then recognising him smiled cautiously. His large gleaming white teeth gave the impression of a Hollywood star made up to look rough and tough. He spoke in reasonably good English. 'And you too, sir.'

'Are you an army man?'

'I am a mountain man. We grow up with guns.'

'But not all grow up to shoot so well.'

'I am pleased they do not. Excuse me please I am on duty.'

'The bouncer?'

'Excuse me?'

'The strong man to throw out trouble makers.'

'Not at all. There are never trouble makers here. I just keep an eye that none enter.' So saying he turned and walked off.

Lance returned to Caroline. 'I am going to tell Jean about Brodie. Stop her wasting any more time on him. Where is she.'

'There, she has just stood up. You had better hurry.'

Lance scampered over; pleased that she had detached herself from her table neighbours. 'Jean. Can I have a word please?'

Jean raised her hands to dissuade him.

'It's important.'

'Right, over here. Be quick, please I have just been called over to that table.'

'It's about Brodie. He is an undertaker. Which explains a lot. Obviously no threat. But he did see blood at the crypt. And he is thinking he should report this to the local police.'

'Damn. That's a nuisance. OK. Thanks.' So saying Jean turned and left him.

'Well, did you see or hear anything suspicious or helpful?' asked Lance after telling Caroline of his brief encounter with Jean.

'Not much. Except that Christophe drove off after the party.'

'So might I. Given a blonde like that.'

'But he left without the blonde.'

'Now that is interesting. I wonder what the blonde is doing.'

'Be serious, Lance. Christophe's movements might merit investigation don't you think?'

'Well, if this evening was typical of his activities close surveillance of him would invite a Peeping Tom charge.'

'So I should maybe undertake that onerous task then.'

'Now who's being serious?'

'So, he left before the end of the party and without the blonde?'

'Yes. Oh and he had a large package in his hand.'

'So, if we cover Christophe that will be about all we can do,' declared Lance when they returned to their chalet.

'Maybe not. If we are going to be really thorough and methodical,' contradicted Caroline. 'How about Kirsty. She goes off on her own. We know less about her than any of the others and she does not look too happy.'

'I never thought of her. Unlikely. But as you say. We must leave no stone etc. But she walks too fast for me.'

'And too far for me. She seems to go miles most days.'

'True,' agreed Lance. 'But not before breakfast. She can't go too far then. She wouldn't have time.'

'Well, in the traditional way we should eliminate her from our enquiries. She is gone less than hour so it can't be too long. I will volunteer to follow her tomorrow morning.'

'Now there's a coincidence. I was going to volunteer you as well.'

Back at the dining chalet next morning they found Albert Brodie in an expansive mood, obviously anxious to make amends for the embarrassment of confronting Lance. Now that they knew his profession he was happy to talk about it. He chose as his opportunity to start when the others round the table were topping each other's tales of the mighty meals they had eaten.

'You're all digging your graves with your knives and forks.' he proclaimed.

Encouraged by the polite laughter, he then regaled them with the Woodie Allen quip 'For three days after you die, your hair and your finger nails continue to grow,' he paused for effect, saw Donna blanch then continued, 'But your telephone calls start to drop off.'

'I suppose you've got to joke in a job like yours,' said Ross, 'To keep from going morbid.'

'Not at all,' Brodie disagreed smiling. 'A pleasant and worthwhile job. We help people at a very difficult time but I could certainly tell you some sad stories.'

'May I ask you a serious question, Mister Brodie?'

'By all means.'

'When we were at Filotosa you explained how much we learned from ancient bodies.'

'Yes, I did.'

'Tell me. Why is it sacrilege to disturb a body say two years after the burial but it is OK to dig up human remains and mess about with them after, say, five hundred years ?'

Albert Brodie was silent for a minute. 'I don't know. I am a practical man. I don't really think much about that sort of thing. And I don't really want to think about it.'

They had all now had enough of this conversation and everyone searched around for another topic to change to, but the next comment didn't take them far from the subject as Kirsty saw Raoul walk past and remarked, 'What a coincidence talking about this. I saw that man coming out of the undertakers yesterday.'

'Probably discussing giving him some business,' said Ross jokingly, but looking pointedly at Lance.

Caroline passed a remark about everyone being unusually lively for breakfast time.

'Maybe because Jean is not here. She is a bit of a dampener. I wonder why she doesn't always come for breakfast,' said Ian.

'She, like the rest of us, can do what we please. I wonder why people don't mind their own business,' said Ross brusquely and left the table.

'I think you've upset him with your talk of funerals. Some people are very sensitive.' Mabel shrugged in disapproval.

'Not at all,' quipped Lance. 'Always interested to hear how the other half dies.'

'Don't you start,' pleaded Caroline.

As they rose from the table Brodie gripped Lance's arm. 'I've been giving our problem some thought.'

Lance looked, and felt, blank.

'A pet.'

Lance looked even more blank.

'That coffin. A facility so that a surviving pet can be added later.'

Lance put on a congratulatory smile. 'Of course. That'll be it. Well done.'

'Good idea too. We learn a little every day.' Brodie strode off, pleased with himself.

Next morning Caroline rose early, watched for Kirsty's departure and followed her up the hill, stealthily to start with then quite openly. She soon lost ground on the younger woman's fast pace up the steep slope but there seem to be but one path so she did not worry. All was quiet except for birdsong. She was beginning to enjoy herself and was wondering if she could coax Lance to do this some morning. Then mingled with the sound of a small waterfall she heard someone sobbing. She crept closer to the sound and saw sitting by the little stream Kirsty with her hands on her face and her shoulders shaking violently.

Caroline straightened up and walked along the path as if to pass the weeping lady.

Kirsty looked up looking started and displeased. 'What are you doing here?'

'Oh, sorry if I have disturbed you. I couldn't sleep and I came up here because I have heard you say how nice it is. I rather hoped we might meet. I don't want to get lost going back.'

Kirsty mopped her face and tried to look more relaxed. 'This is as far as I come. Sit down and we can go back together.'

'Thank you. That's very kind of you.' She was quiet for a few minutes and enjoyed the sound of the running water. When it seemed to her that Kirsty had regained her composure she spoke softly.

'You were sobbing. Look if you are mourning or something. I'll go and leave you in peace.'

Her gentle words set Kirsty's weeping off again and Caroline just waited for the distressed woman to speak again.

After some time she blew her nose then braced herself. 'Thank you. No, I'm not mourning. Or if I am, I'm mourning for myself.' She choked back another sob. 'I start a course of Chemotherapy when I get back. I am hopeless. Lots of people are so brave about this.'

She shook her head. 'I want to be brave but I have nobody to be brave to. That sounds pathetic, doesn't it?'

'Not at all.'

'You see I am single, my parents are gone, I have no sisters or brothers, I have just changed my job, a good job but in a new town so I don't even know my colleagues. I know I should be brave and I am sure I could be – but I have no one to be brave in front of.' She shook her head disparaging herself. 'Really pathetic.'

'No. I think I understand.'

'I feel a little better just having talked to you. I haven't talked to anyone else about this except the doctors. Don't tell the others please. I don't want sympathy.'

'I promise. I won't even tell Lance.'

'I envy you and Lance. You seem to have a wonderful relationship.'

'It's pretty good. But don't tell Lance I said that. He already thinks he's God's gift to me.'

Kirsty's mouth relaxed into a little smile.

A shaft of light from the rising sun peeped round a small cloud and highlighted a profusion of daffodils. A gentle Mexican wave ran along the golden blooms as they responded to the light breeze and performed their stiff stemmed Wordsworthian dance; swaying but not bending. The ladies watched in silence.

After a few minutes Kirsty scrambled to her feet, took Caroline's hand and said. 'Let's go get some breakfast.'

Just as they were about to enter the villas Kirsty reached down into a small stream and splashed water on her face.

She looked reasonably composed when they sat down at the breakfast table.

Caroline did not.

CHAPTER EIGHTEEN

Lance was just heading to the breakfast chalet when Caroline returned. Caroline took him by the hand and told him quietly but very firmly that Kirsty was all right and that she would tell him about it some day. An attempt by Lance to pursue the subject was emphatically squashed. Caroline sat beside Kirsty..

Breakfast was a subdued affair. All agreed enthusiastically that it had been a splendid spread with great entertainment but most of them agreed that they had overdone it a bit and they vied in their description of the strength of the deadly brew they had been unwise enough to consume. Kirsty seemed the only not moaning and the Brodies were absent.

'Are you hardened to this sort of thing, Kirsty,' asked Ross.

'Not at all,' scoffed Kirsty. 'I was wise enough to leave early. I enjoyed it but I knew when I had had enough.'

Ian held his head and groaned. 'I wish you had taken me with you.'

'Now there's a treat you missed, Kirsty,' quipped Ross.

Kirsty blushed. 'I realized this morning just what a good night it must have been. I saw the big man Raoul with a great bundle over his shoulder heading out of the villas. It looked like a drunk being taken off the premises.'

'The lovely things you see if you get up early enough.'

'That's true, Ross but you won't see anything messy if you get up later. Raoul makes sure nothing embarrassing to the sisters is about when the guests get up.' So saying Donna offered coffee. 'If this were later in the day I would offer you miserable lot a drink to cheer you up.'

'Don't. I'm never going to drink again,' moaned Ian.

Ross rose. 'I'm off to bed.'

Ian followed him sluggishly.

'Lovely day. I think I'll take a long walk this morning.' Kirsty rose and headed briskly towards the exit.

Left alone Caroline and Lance speculated on what had kept the Brodies away. 'I don't think they were drinking a lot.'

'Gone to a grave that looks better in the early morning light perhaps.'

'We must tell Jean the whole story about Bones – sorry – Albert Brodie. She seemed in a hurry last night.'

It was two hours before they chanced on her walking towards her chalet. They dashed round a flower bed and headed her off.

'Ah Jean,' greeted Lance. 'We wanted to have a chat with you.'

'About.'

'Brodie. I can tell you all about him. Save you time.'

'A bit late. Who else did you tell about him thinking about going to the police?'

'No one.' Then added. 'Except Caroline of course.'

'Are you sure?'

'Absolutely. Why.'

'Because he was found dead among the villas this morning.' Jean strode off before they could say another word.

'Well, well. Poor old Albert. A nut case but he didn't deserve that.'

'Deserve what,' asked Caroline. 'You sound as if you assume he was killed. He could have just died.'

'Yes, he could. Do you think so?'

'No. I must admit I don't. I don't like the idea that this happened so soon after you learned that he was thinking of going to the police.'

'And I passed on that information.'

'To Jean.'

'I wonder if she passed it on.'

'To whom? I can't imagine a British organization could be that ruthless.'

'What newspapers do you read? The Beano. This means that I ---'

Caroline interrupted him. 'This must be something really big whether it was the goodies or the baddies who did him in.'

'You mean big enough to justify this – and Jean One.'

'Yes. Big money. But let's not jump our guns. Sorry badly worded. We don't know he was killed. Whatever happened we should find Mabel and have a word with her. Killed or died she will need a bit of comfort.'

Later that day they found Mabel sitting on an out of the way bench gazing out towards the sea. She was dressed in dark clothes – but she was always dressed in dark clothes.

Lance and Caroline sat down quietly beside her and said nothing for a few minutes.

Caroline broke the silence gently, 'We are so sorry.'

Mabel did not respond.

After a time Lance spoke up. 'We can't think why this has happened.'

'I don't care why it happened. It doesn't make any difference who, why or how.'

'Don't you want – closure?'

'I don't know what that means. Tell me.'

'I must confess I don't know either. I think it's a TV word.'

'He was a good man,' said Mabel in a way which made it sound like an entirely negative quality.

'Can we help in any way?' asked Caroline.

'Thank you. I don't think so. Kirsty has offered, in fact insisted, that she will travel home with me. So she is going to come away early and help me home. We had a long chat and she did cheer me up a bit. Must be good to be carefree. She is a real nice lass.'

'Yes she is, isn't she.' Caroline whispered.

'When I get him home our staff will look after him.'

'Very well I'm sure.'

Lance asked, 'What will you do now?'

Mabel thought for a few moments. 'I have been thinking about that. I would like to train to be a midwife. If they will have me.' She paused. 'See the world from the other end, so to speak.' She half smiled.

Caroline looked at Mabel's soft, calm face. 'I think you would make a fine midwife.'

'Thanks.' Mabel now really smiled.

They never saw her or Kirsty again.

'I suppose she will sell the business as a going concern,' suggested Lance in an effort to lighten the gloom.'

'Shut up,' suggested Caroline.

CHAPTER NINETEEN

As a grim faced Lance prepared for his drive up the mountains, Caroline agreed to seek out Jean Two if he did not reappear in two hours and report to her where he had gone; as an insurance. They were serious behind the banter.

'Bernard the Bus was probably just taking some scones up to an old aunt,' suggested Caroline.

'I hope so. I see my part in this enterprise from now on as eliminating the irrelevant while you are hot on the scent, daring, defiant and of course, beautiful. That's the kind of story I like.'

'I'll see if I can find somebody to defy while you're enjoying yourself.'

But as Lance climbed into the car she whispered, 'Be careful.'

Lance had no difficulty finding the road. It was the only one leading off to the left and, as Ross had said, the road was treeless and open. No one could travel along it furtively. You could see for miles ahead.

All the more of a surprise it was then when Lance, rounding the slightest of bends, found a man standing in the middle of the road waving him down. He instantly recognised Raoul and his first instinct was to drive straight on and make him jump for it. But two thoughts flashed simultaneously into his mind; that the big man would not jump - and that he would inevitably meet him again later. He stopped and summoned up a smile.

'My bike. It has given up. It is a small bike for such a hill.'

'And for such a load,' quipped Lance to make himself feel better.

Raoul smiled and nodded. 'I have to go to the end of the road - a short visit. Could I accompany you?'

'By all means. Climb in.'

Raoul squeezed in to the small car and hunched forward, peering ahead. Just as Lance was about to ask the same question, Raoul spoke. 'What brings you up this road?'

Trying hard to hide his distaste for the narrow, unmade track as they jolted along, he lied, 'I just like driving about by myself. Roads I have not been on before. You know? There are always surprises.'

'Some of these roads are dangerous.'

Lance explained carefully, 'I always tell Caroline exactly where I'm going. She will be up here like a shot if I am late in returning, probably with half of the Corsican police force. She fusses,' he added. 'And you. What brings you up here? Visiting a remote aunt or something?'

Raoul looked puzzled. 'No. Not that. A man causes trouble to the sisters and anyone who causes trouble to them causes trouble to me. He comes up here. I wonder why.'

They drove on in silence. As they rounded a bend, after a long desolate, uninhabited stretch of road, a large barn type building, grey and inconspicuous, stood, alone and almost hidden, backed right up against a cliff face. In front of it stretched a large flat expanse; one of the rare level areas they had seen on the island.. There was no sign of any other vehicle near the building. Lance drew up about fifty yards from it, just where the road ended and the flat ground opened out. They paused but there was no reaction from the barn. Lance switched off the engine and they listened; still no sign of life. Raoul swung his bulk from the car. He crouched and crept cautiously towards the only door. He knocked and slid away from the opening, ready to pounce on anyone who came out. There was still no response. He tried the door. It was locked. He circled the building and reappeared at the front shaking his head. He then picked up a huge stone, with only a little grunt, and hurtled it through a boarded up window. It yielded with a cracking of wood and shattering of glass. Raoul indicated to Lance to come over. Now curious but still nervous, Lance walked slowly to him.

'I must know what's inside. Please?'

The huge man picked Lance up before he could agree or otherwise, balanced him by his foot momentarily then propelled him through the jagged opening. Lance tucked in his arms to avoid the shards of glass and landed unhurt but badly shaken on an earthen floor. He limped to the door but could not open it from the inside. He shouted out. 'I can't open it. Must be locked from your side.' He looked around then shouted. 'Just stacks of packing cases in here.'

'I will come.' Raoul had much greater difficulty squeezing his own great body through the window. As he was struggling, Lance had a quick look round to make sure they were the only occupants before turning to help him through and down. Raoul was cut but seemed unconcerned. Lance now saw that the barn was almost filled with crates of good quality, obviously constructed to be waterproof and amenable to robust handling. They looked important. He decided to go along with whatever Raoul had in mind. The adrenalin was now flowing and he felt at last he might learn something useful.

They had just bent over to examine the boxes when they heard the scream of tyres. Raoul rushed straight to the window and seeing the driver dismount with a rifle in his hands shot twice at the approaching man with a hand gun. The driver yelped and bolted back into a jeep and drove off as fast as he could.

'Quick,' shouted Raoul. He picked up a jemmy like implement which hung on the wall and forced open one of the cases. They saw rows and rows of gleaming rifles, carefully stacked and shining new.

'Bring the car nearer.' The big man was lifting out some of the rifles.

Lance hurried to the door. The interior bolts were not in place but the door would not budge. Raoul rushed over and shot twice at the lock; the bullets came back past them dangerously close. He then raised a large foot and kicked the sole of his boot against the door with an almighty thump. It swung open. Lance sped through and ran towards the car. He hadn't gone five paces when a bullet whined past him. He dived to the ground, somersaulted twice and scrambled desperately along the ground back to the doorway, being closely followed by spurts of earth. Raoul rushed over to the window and looked out. Another shot rang out.

'Over there. In that bush.' He pointed to a scruffy lump of vegetation hundreds of yards away. Yet another shot and he withdrew his head quickly.

Raoul turned back to the opened case and picked out two rifles then searched around. He found what he wanted and tore at another case and produced some ammunition. He tossed a rifle and a box of ammunition to Lance who, calling back memories of old skills, loaded the firearm and stuffed some bullets in his pockets.

They now rushed around checking the building and found that the door just kicked in was the only way out: the shattered window was too awkward for a quick exit and directly in the sights of the sniper. But even the door, they reckoned, would necessitate their pausing in the line of fire too long. In turns they snatched a quick look out at the sniper's bush to plan their next move but every time either of them peeped a head from the barn a shot ricocheted off the stone wall.

They were pinned down. The fire initiative is lost - Lance recalled the military phrase. He looked around for a route to perform a flanking move on the marksman. There was none. The cliff rose straight up at the back of the barn. In front and to the side the ground was flat, sandy and stony; small stones, not rocks which might have provided some cover. The shrubs were sparse and stunted. They could not take a step without exposing themselves. They had cover in the barn - they had none if they moved out of it. The marksman was saving his ammunition - he only shot when they showed themselves.

'He can hold us here and wait for reinforcements,' growled Raoul.

'And you. Do you have reinforcements?'

The big man shook his head.

After a time Raoul turned to Lance and growled, 'You can shoot?' Lance nodded. 'I can remember. With this rifle could you hit that man from here?'

Lance weighed the fine modern piece in his hand and looked at it lovingly. He felt confident that he could use it effectively. He looked out, showing just the top of his head. The sniper did not fire. He withdrew. and thought for a time, glanced out again, shook his head and said, 'No. It's too far.'

'I think so too,' agreed Raoul.

Lance felt a surge of despair - they were trapped, probably by people who had already murdered.

Raoul stood up; his face grim. 'Come then. He has the same rifle, exactly the same. He cannot hit us from there.' He picked up his rifle and walked towards the door. 'Except perhaps a lucky shot!'

The big man walked calmly out of the door with no ducking or dodging. Two shots rung out and Lance could hear the bullets strike the stone barn and scream into the air.

'I think we may be better shots,' shouted the big man as he stopped about thirty yards out, lay down, took careful aim and fired. He stood up and started walking forward again.

Lance hurried out and caught up with Raoul, who beckoned him to keep a distance apart. The sand spurted up about five yards from Lance's feet. He sidled back a little closer. After a further thirty paces they both lay down and shot. The sniper blazed off a few shots.

Again, Raoul rose and strode forward holding himself erect and contemptuous. Lance did likewise with just a little surreptitious crouch. The shots were now passing frighteningly close.

Twice more they did this and the shots were now just missing. Then a bullet having hit a rock tore through Lance's trouser leg on the deflection and a patch of blood appeared on the lightly coloured cloth.

'A lucky shot,' hissed Lance.

Raoul smiled as his companion walked on.

They lay down. Lance said, 'Both together this time.'

Lance remembered to squeeze the trigger gently. Two shots cracked out. They looked up. Something was moving from the distant bush. They saw the figure of a man leave the shelter of the bush and scramble away on all fours, then rise and flee as fast as he could.

They sent a couple of shots after him. A vehicle started up in the distance.

Raoul laughed. 'I thought it would be so.'

Lance had an urge to shake the hand of this remarkable man but, as his own hand was already shaking, he thought this might undermine the regard reflected in the big man's smile. He confined himself to a Clint Eastwood nod and grunt.

They rushed back into the barn, took some examples from the armoury, backed the car up to the door and loaded it. Without asking Raoul squeezed himself into the driver's seat and drove off on a rough stony track. The big man handled the car with an impatient skill. They both forgot their respective welling blood.

After a mile of bumping they rejoined the road and shortly afterwards Raoul pulled up where he had left his motorcycle.

He took some rifles and ammunition and strapped them to his bike and left one weapon and a box of ammunition with Lance. He straddled the bike and pushed off down the hill. As soon as he engaged gear it sprang to life. The enormous pressure of Raoul's gravity brought forth of scream of protest from the small machine.

He shouted back over the noise. 'I suggest you change your car.' Then even more loudly, 'And don't report this or I will break your neck - slowly.' He drove off without a backward glance.

CHAPTER TWENTY

Lance was driving slowly down hill trying to give his pulse a chance to ease off before he met Caroline, then he looked at his watch and realised he would have to put his foot down to be back in the agreed two hours. In view of Raoul's parting words he parked the car in a wooded area near the resort and limped home. So it was, when Caroline did see him again he was agitated, stressed and ragged - and he had a blood stained trouser leg. It was therefore difficult to put on the casual act he had been rehearsing on the way down.

She gasped and hauled him into the chalet. 'Take these trousers off.'

'I was hoping you were going to say that.'

'Not grape juice this time.'

Caroline went for a clean cloth and put a kettle on. She rubbed at the periphery of the bloodstain and gradually worked her way in. To her great relief she had reduced the bloodstain to a small area before there was any sign of a wound. Now at Lance's repeated suggestion she started taking it more and more gently. When all was revealed a crimson slash about quarter of an inch thick, two inches long and scarcely any depth was the extent of the damage. In spite of the protests that it was unnecessary, Caroline cleaned it thoroughly with piping hot water. She then bandaged it neatly.

She leaned back, still looking worried. 'Go on, tell me it was a thorn.'

Lance recounted the tale and could sense Caroline mentally discounting his heroic bits.

'And what has this all to do with Jean?'

'I haven't the foggiest idea.'

'Right, to bed with you. That's bound to have been a shock to the system even for an action man like you. So - no nonsense. Off you go.'

'I love it when you're dominating.'

'I'll remember that.'

Caroline gave Lance more than two hours in bed. She took his pulse every ten minutes and found that it soon returned to normal. She was sure the wound was not serious but was determined to go to the doctor at the slightest sign of infection.

There was nothing more she could do for him so, having taken Raoul's warning more seriously than did Lance, she took the car down to the hirer and changed it. She smiled sweetly and said she didn't like the colour. When she got back she went to the bathroom for a face cloth to wipe Lance's brow. Not necessary, she thought, but a gesture. Then she saw under Lance's electric razor a small sheet of paper. She picked it up and on it were scribbled in block capitals the words, 'KEEP OUT OF THIS OR YOUR WIFE WILL MEET WITH AN ACCIDENT.' She looked at it for a long time, rereading it, her knees shaking, then she tore it up into tiny pieces and dropped it into the waste bin.

She woke Lance with a cup of tea and a patisserie knowing this would do him as much good as anything.

'Thank you. Just what I need. I have a feeling I may have to be fairly active in the near future. Everything seems to be coming to a head.'

'Well then, you'll need this.' Caroline brought him a hat; he had returned from the hills without his. They set off to test the injured leg. It was painful but in no way restricted his movement and after a few paces he was striding out again.

'OK, I get the message. You feel fine. But you didn't walk as fast as this before you were wounded.' Caroline complained.

Lance slowed down then said, thoughtfully, 'I wonder if it is arms smugglers they're after. If so, it's big and it's nasty.'

'Well, if British police are involved there must be British arms involved.'

'Would be. I once read that if some little people are being shot by anyone with enough money to buy guns, anywhere in the world, it will likely be by British, American, French or Russian guns. And they are the upholders of world peace. I don't understand.'

'Nor do I. Except - British jobs. Is that justification? But it's a rotten trade whoever's doing it. Go to Puerto Banus and you will see yachts with helipads built in reputedly owned by arms dealers. Whether they are legal or not I don't like the idea of someone making huge profits out of that. I hope Jean Two's team blows them apart whatever nationality is involved - and I hope we've been of some help to her.'

'Agreed. Why do all these wee civil wars in countries where they can't afford enough food never run out of bullets?' Caroline was trying hard to reinforce her resolve.

'Given today's thinking we would have probably sold Gatling guns to the Zulus and that would have changed history.' Lance was getting irritable and impatient. 'Look darling, we've eliminated Ross and Brodie has been elimnated. Let's have a closer look at Christophe. He's up to something.'

'I don't trust him either. A smoothy. He's the sort of man who would rub sugar in your wounds.' Caroline now consulted her list. 'He sometimes goes shopping at this time.'

Lance started to head towards the little delicatessen where they bought their picnic supplies.

Caroline tugged him in the opposite direction. 'In the supermarket.'

Lance grunted his disapproval. He thought that getting away from supermarkets was an important constituent of a break from home ground; holiday resorts should have quaint little crowded stores with the scents of real food heavy in the air, manned by a fat pleasant proprietor who smiled in recognition if you entered the store a second time.

So they went shopping in the supermarket. They chose some local pate; on Caroline's insistence they turned down the blackbird, then some crusty bread and a bottle of white wine. They planned to cool this in a mountain stream, a stream somewhat nearer the foot of the hills than on their last experience on the mountains.

As they queued to pay at the check out desk, Caroline nodded towards the front of the line. 'Look, talk of the devil. There's Christophe in front of us. Looks very ordinary and domestic in a supermarket queue.'

Christophe stood there, elegant as always, in a coffee coloured linen jacket and trousers a shade lighter.

'But still not exactly angelic. What's he buying?' asked Lance.

'Can't be anything very ominous in here. Except maybe,' she paused for effect, 'the cornflakes.' Lance looked bewildered.

Caroline continued. 'They're giving away plastic guns. Choice of colour. Bet he picks a black one.'

'Don't take the micky,' protested Lance. 'You never know where or when we might pick up a clue.' He was now watching Christophe closely.

There were three customers lined up to pay between them and Christophe, so they could not follow him when he left the store. They had an interminable wait behind the woman immediately in front who was scrambling in her purse under a large sign proclaiming 'Use our store credit card and save time.' With a flourish she eventually produced her store credit card and shortly they were free. As they left the pay desk Lance tripped and stopped to tie his laces.

Caroline looked on in amazement. Lance snapped. 'Pop your eyes back in your head. You'll draw attention to us.'

'I'll draw attention to us!' It was a cross between a whisper and a scream. 'And you won't? Haven't you noticed your shoes don't have laces? Who do you think you are - Marcel Marceux?'

'Come with me.' Lance straightened up and hurried her outside and down to the wine bar.

'Ah, the revelation place. What are you going to reveal this time?'

'These.' He placed four crumpled checkout receipts on the table. 'One of these was dropped by Christophe. You never know. Might learn something.'

'There's the bin outside his chalet too.'

'Don't be sarcastic. Take two and look.'

'Right.' She smoothed one out. 'Cleaning fluid, detergent and brillo pads. I don't think this is his, somehow.'

Lance now read from one. 'Bon bons, jam, bread, butter and three kinds of cheese and - wait for it - a packet of cornflakes.'

They laughed.

Caroline eyes widened and her finger stopped halfway down the next list. 'Campari!'

'Let me see.' Lance shouted and grabbed the slip. 'It must be him. Campari. This is our breakthrough.'

'Read on,' instructed Caroline.

'Campari, shaving soap, paper hankies, toilet roll and sun lotion. Well, what do you make of that?'

'To start with the simplest. Shaving soap, hankies and sun oil approved. But we get toilet rolls provided at the chalets. Right?'

'Agreed. Another puzzle. And why does he buy Campari when he can get it at the bar?'

'Cheaper.'

'Right. Anyway we now know he is the Campari drinker. He must have been with her around the time she died.'

CHAPTER TWENTY ONE

A strong pleasant smell reached Lance and Caroline from the great open fireplace although they had selected a table at the other end of the long room to avoid the heat as it was still warm outside though the sun was setting; it was the fragrance of the sea. As they looked at the huge handwritten menu their minds were already made up; the giant crayfish grilling over the flames advertised themselves. They laid down the cards and looked around. Three old cottages had been knocked together making a long narrow dining room. Whitewashed walls gave it an air of spaciousness.

It had been a good recommendation, even if the advice had not been sought with the food or the ambience principally in mind. On one evening each week the girls did not cook and the guests were expected to make their own arrangements. It gave the girls a night off, it gave the holiday makers a chance to sample the local hostelries and, importantly, it gave Lance and Caroline a chance, they hoped, to meet with the elusive sisters.

Caroline, in asking for Meryl's advice, had said, 'Where, for instance, would the sisters go if they were dining out?' She was sure that the sisters were somewhere near the heart of the deadly drama.

'Almost always the Berangeria. It's their favourite. It's lovely. I've been there once. In fact, I would go there more often except that I don't want to bump into the sisters on my night off. Like to relax. And it's a bit pricey.'

So they had found themselves here and, adopting Lance's one and only principle of detecting practice, had arrived early so that they were not suspected of following. They were filling in the time pleasantly sipping Myrrt, the clear, sweet scented liqueur distilled from myrtle, and breathing in the flavours of the food in prospect. The restaurant was alongside a rough road perched precariously on a cliff top overlooking the darkening sea. The sun was pointing a flaming finger straight at them across the water and tingeing the underside of the wisps of cloud with fire.

The narrowness of the room accentuated the girth of the plump lady overseeing the grill and that of her equally rotund husband both of whom dashed hither and thither with plates, bowls, tureens and beaming faces.

The doorways were built in proportion to the rooms and Lance and Caroline watched fascinated as they saw how expertly the two hurrying hosts managed, with deft pauses, to avoid meeting at these bottlenecks.

They toyed with their drinks for a long time then, for appearances sake, but also because they were starting to drool, they ordered. They were now worried that their prey was not going to appear this evening although somewhat reassured by the fact that, even though the restaurant was now filling up, there were still some vacant tables, each with a reserved notice.

They were half way through their crayfish, which even in the interests of the grim purpose of their visit they refused to eat slowly and let go cold, when the sisters appeared. By the way the host rushed over and ushered them to the prime table in the corner, which had windows all round, it was obvious that they were valued customers. Madame also left her leaping flames and bustled over to kiss them each on both cheeks.

The sisters were dressed soberly from the waist down in long black skirts but their ample bosoms were decorated with colourful blouses. They sat down and it seemed that their worries, and they had looked worried when they entered, left them as they sunk down on their chairs and relaxed in the friendly and familiar place. They did not even glance at the menu but sat quietly looking around the, now well filled, room exchanging friendly nods with some of the other guests and occasionally admiring the view out of the window. They whispered to each other and smiled. Rhoda reached forward and squeezed Mona's hand.

'They've had a quarrel.' Caroline spoke quietly. 'I can tell. Rhoda looks just like you do when you're trying to get back into my good books.'

'Well, I hope she has better luck.'

Lance and Caroline lingered over a delicious sweet and sipped the one glass of wine they were allowing themselves in view of the narrow winding road back to Villamaquis. They agreed, as they were at the extreme end of the long room, that they would have to stop at the sisters' table and greet them if they were to make the contact they desired. The sisters would not be coming their way.

Thinking, with their table cleared and their glasses empty, that they had dawdled long enough, Lance called to the patron for the bill. He abetted them in their desire to linger by bringing a bottle of yellow liqueur with a frond of vegetation in it and insisting that they have a glass of this speciality of the house, on the house. He obviously wished to make them feel welcome and chatted cheerfully about Britain and told them of the recent visitors to his restaurant from there, pointing out some reasonably well known names in the visitor's book. They encouraged him in this conversation, not only to pass time, but because they were genuinely enjoying his friendly chat. Eventually his others duties called him away.

As the route to the exit did not take them close enough to the table occupied by the sisters Caroline went to the toilet and stopped at their table on her way back. She chatted to them for a time then signalled for Lance to come over.

'These ladies invite us to join them for a drink before we go.'

Lance put on a doubtful look. 'That is very kind of you. By all means you have a drink, Caroline. I have to drive back down that hill.'

Mona was already gesturing to the patron and he came bustling over.

'Please sit down. We were just about to have a little drink ourselves to round off our evening. Having Champagne here is part of the evenings entertainment and we certainly cannot drink a bottle by ourselves so we are asking for your assistance.'

They sat down and Lance, aware of the still burning sensation of the patron's liqueur, said that he would have a mineral water.

'Nonsense.' proclaimed Rhoda. 'You will leave your car here and return with us. We will have someone drive you here to pick it up your car tomorrow morning.'

Lance and Caroline protested but not too vigorously. They sat down and soon relaxed as the sisters seemed genuinely pleased to see them. Lance had the feeling that their presence was postponing a disagreement.

They talked about the island, the weather and the resort until the host came over with the bottle of Champagne.

'Now watch this,' said Rhoda her eyes wide.

The plump man now took a short slightly curved sword from the wall, held the Champagne bottle firmly with the other hand then, with a great flourish, struck the bottle obliquely on the base of the neck. To a round of applause from the other diners who had been watching, some knowing what was going to happen, the top of the bottle fell to the floor and the champagne bubbles welled from the neatly severed neck. Lance and Caroline joined in the applause.

The patron bowed to the table then turned and bowed to the others in the room. He passed the bottle neck with the cork still in it, to Rhoda who immediately passed it to Caroline who accepted it with a beaming smile and a bow to the host. She tucked the souvenir into her handbag.

The table was cleared and they settled down to enjoy the Champagne. After Lance and Caroline had paid many compliments to the sisters on the service and facilities at Villamaquis, the sisters recounted how they had come to start their enterprise and laughed at the stories of hotels which were still artists impressions when the holiday makers arrived, waterless swimming pools, disappearing buses and couriers more interested in getting into each other's bed than seeing that their clients had somewhere to sleep, all of which they had experienced in their previous careers working for a tour organiser.

'I was told once,' said Rhoda, 'Listen carefully and sympathetically to any complaint, note it, then forget it and deny any recollection of it.'

'Of course, it was big business,' added Mona. 'We intend to stay small.'

They prided themselves that nothing like that happened to any of their clients. It was on the tip of Lance's tongue to ask how they recorded the occasions when one of their clients disappeared even more completely than the aforementioned buses, but realised that that line of approach would get him nowhere. He certainly could not disagree with their boast that they gave their clients freedom.

'Did you ever hear what caused the explosion up in the hills? We looked at a map and it seemed to come from the village of Olmacci.' Lance asked instead.

'That's a grape growing area. I can't think what could blow up. I don't think there is anything very dangerous in the wine making process,' said Mona.

'Unless something fermented too quickly,' suggested Rhoda.

Mona scoffed and Lance asked if it could have been bandits.

'No,' answered Mona. 'There was evidently a big clear out back in the nineteen thirties and the bandits were virtually wiped out. There are some nationalists but we don't hear much from them, perhaps we're too near the Foreign Legion base in Bonifacio.'

'Are there smugglers in the hills?' asked Caroline. 'No one could catch them up there.'

Mona scowled. 'We have our fair share of all types of modern criminals, but I don't think we have more that our share. We have a good police force.'

'No, I'm sure that's so. The world is a dreadful place. You do well to provide a little haven.'

A delighted Mona beamed. 'We try.'

'Like all good things it, no doubt, has to be guarded. It's an unfortunate fact that wherever you're enjoying yourself these days, you always see a guard of some sort.'

'Is this so obvious?' Rhoda sounded disappointed.

'Not more so than usual. We have bouncers outside most London pubs now.'

'But Raoul does look a bit overpowering. I keep saying so to Rhoda.' Mona looked at her sister.

'But he is effective, you must admit. You know of course, Mister Lockhart that we provide free cycles for the use of our guests to ride around the area. Well, some get mislaid, some get stolen and others are left in the village by guests who realise that cycling downhill is more fun than cycling uphill. But all of these bikes find their way back to us. No one would risk Raoul hearing of any of them having one of our cycles. I don't know why you still don't trust him, Mona.'

'I don't trust him because he's in the protection racket. If we didn't employ him bad things would happen to us.'

'Nonsense Mona. We've been over this so many times. He put his application for the job to us badly - too strongly. But his English is not too good.'

'You may be right, dear sister, but I sometimes think it is we who are protecting him. He uses our place as his refuge. He is not what he seems. He keeps strange company. And as you know he can upset people who are very important to us. Particularly when he's trying to be helpful.' This was directed at Rhoda, but now she turned to Lance. 'Do you find him intimidating, Mister Lockhart?'

'Not at all. He is always polite and it's reassuring to think he's on our side. He is a powerful man. Tell me? I've often wondered, why does he not bring his bike into the villas?'

'To check that our watchmen are not sleeping on the job. Creeps up on them.' answered Rhoda.

'And he's had his bike vandalised. Sugar in the petrol. Tyres cut. I don't like people with enemies about the place,' said Mona emphatically.

'I think he could look after himself,' ventured Lance.

Rhoda smiled and looked at Mona. 'He is not your real enemy, and you know it.'

'He is a roughneck,' snapped Mona. She turned to Caroline and nodded towards Rhoda. 'Always had a weakness for strong men. Fell for Raoul when she saw him bend a steel bar round his neck. Show off.'

Rhoda scowled.

Caroline changed the subject by asking about the history of the Berangeria and the sisters soon forgot their disagreement and vied in their praises of the restaurant and the couple who owned it. It had only been converted five years ago but was already renowned in the island.

Tables had to be booked weeks ahead - except if you phoned from Villamaquis.

The meal, the champagne and the soft upholstery overwhelmed Lance and he fell asleep in the large car in which they were driven home. He tumbled into bed hoping to think only of the lovely meal but before he fell asleep again, he said to Caroline. 'Someone is killed in the explosion yet no-one knows of it. It takes a big man to cover up that.' Caroline grunted in agreement but dozed off almost immediately.

It was at breakfast the next morning that the bent steel bar came back to his mind. They now knew who had been in the old stone building.

CHAPTER TWENTY NINE

As they walked away from the breakfast table Caroline took Lance over to a patch of high shrubbery. 'When you were talking to your pal yesterday I heard one of the gardeners complaining to Raoul about someone having messed up one of his tools. He was angry, going to complain to Mona so that he did not get the blame. Raoul said he would take it and report the matter. When the gardener was gone he had glanced over towards the office, looked apprehensive, shrugged and then tossed whatever it was into that waste bin. I thought it might possibly be of interest to have a look.'

They looked. A badly damaged pair of secateurs nestled amongst the assorted rubbish.

'They've been used on something too tough for them.'

'Like wire fencing?'

They went immediately to the place where they thought the body must have been taken over the fence. They checked much more closely than they had done previously and found that the fence had indeed been breached. The main ragged cut was along the base of the fence and had been hidden by the simple ploy of raising the level of the dry earth so that the join was completely hidden. Where the wire must have been folded back it was almost invisibly mended where it was attached to the supporting posts. All of this exactly where they had been speculating about how anybody could get a body over such a high barrier. They strolled back to the villas wondering what their next move should be.

Lance's leg had stiffened up a little during the night so they walked leisurely about the villas not saying anything, both baffled and at a loss as to what to say or do next. Christophe stood on his verandah looking worried. They stopped and, keeping out of his sight, observed him as they did now each time their paths had crossed since the Campari revelation. This time Caroline's hand tightened on Lance's arm.

'Look.'

'I'm looking.'

'Anything familiar?'

'Of course. We've seen him every day.'

'Look. The profile. The worried look.'

'I'm not with you.'

'Prince Charming.'

'Don't start that again.'

'Just look. Think back. The Sleeping Beauty. It was him. The Prince.'

Lance looked intently at the serious faced man. 'You know, you could be right.'

They hurried on and sat down on their favourite chairs by the tennis courts. Lance did not even glance at the four young ladies battling it out with yellow balls.

'Imagine, those festive crowds were cheering a corpse going past.'

'Don't Lance, please.'

'What does this make of the bloodstains over by the fence? The track in the maquis? The body in the coffin?'

'A false trail. If so, which one is false? Or another body. I don't know.'

'Think about Sleeping Beauty's face. Was it Jean?'

'I can't recall it. Certainly we didn't see her hair. There was a sort of snood thing over it.'

'Yes. He would want to hide the hair. The face was white. Powdered I thought. Lots of make up.'

'But it could have been her.'

'It could have been her.'

Lance was quiet for a few moments then he spoke seriously. 'I'm going to confront him. Sleeping Beauty and Campari. But first I must write a couple of letters. Bear with me.'

They returned to the chalet and Lance hurriedly wrote the first of his letters.

'Post this please, while I write the next one. I'll explain as we go along. Hurry. We must catch him now before he disappears or gets up to more villainy.'

When Caroline returned, she had gone to the village rather than trust the Villamaquis post box, Lance was waiting impatiently.

'Your other letter?' asked Caroline.

'Attended to. Look, I think we should both go and speak to Christophe. He will realise if I bring you, I must be very confident.'

'And are you?'

'I'm trying. Let's go.'

Christophe was on his verandah but sitting down now, still looking worried. He rose as they approached.

'May we have a word?' asked Lance.

'Of course. Do be seated.' The Frenchman pulled a chair forward for Caroline and putting a hand on her waist guided her into it. 'This is a pleasant surprise, Caroline.'

'No, it isn't.' Lance started abrasively. He remained standing to gain a psychological and perhaps physical advantage. 'It is unpleasant. I will come straight to the point. I - we have - indications that you are involved in a murder. We do not wish to look foolish so, before taking any action, we are giving you the chance to disprove it.'

Christophe looked at them in amazement. 'What are you? Not police. They would never behave in this stupid manner. Go away or I will call them.'

'May we stay while you do so?'

Christophe looked steadily at Lance. 'What do you want?'

Lance returned the gaze equally unwavering. 'I want to know where the body of Jean Faulds is - and I want to know who killed her.'

'She is in your group. You are better able to know where she is than I am.'

'The original Jean Faulds.'

'There are two?'

'Yes. And well you know it. I want to know what happened to her. And what your involvement is – was?'

'Just that. And how do you propose to find that out?'

'You will tell us what you know.'

Christophe laughed. 'And if I am a dangerous killer why don't I just kill you?'

'You might, but hear this first - I've not been very original but I have been careful. I have posted a letter to the police telling them where I have hidden details of a murder which, of course, includes the evidence implicating you. If I get back in time after having been reassured by you I can destroy that hidden document and I will only have wasted, no doubt valuable, police time.'

'And this evidence?' Christophe was still mocking.

'Many indicators pointing to you. Very persuasive indicators. So we will need proof, not words. I will not tell you all we know , of course, but - we would like to find the Sleeping Beauty.'

For the first time Christophe looked taken aback. He was quiet and deep in thought for a long time. Lance did not interrupt him. When he spoke again he sounded angry. 'You are a nuisance. I have little time to spare. I cannot fool around. I can take you to the body and I can prove to you that I did not kill her. But you must do it my way. Precisely. You have your insurance policy. I must also safeguard myself. Then we must both take the risk.'

'Agreed,' Lance's voice was firm but he reached for Caroline's hand. He desperately wanted to get at the truth he did not really want to see the body.

CHAPTER TWENTY THREE

'Naked' Lance exploded.

'Naked,' repeated Christophe firmly.

'I'm not going anywhere, naked.'

'If you wish the whereabouts of the body of Jean Faulds to know, you must do this. We will meet on the Prammis beach where all will be naked. You will not be conspicuous.'

'He will not be conspicuous,' laughed Caroline, who was enjoying herself.

'You keep out of this. But why? Why cannot we just go there now - like this?'

'Because I trust no-one. You might be kitted out like your James Bond.'

'But getting away from the beach. I can't go from the beach, to - to wherever, in the nude. No, you're not on.'

'I will have clothes for you. For when we meet. Clothes with no hidden surprises. It is simple. If you have nothing to hide.'

Lance turned on his grinning wife. 'One word from you and I'll thump you.'

'Come now. Is this so difficult? You would in fact stand out if you did wear clothes on that beach.'

'So you will also be unclad.'

'Of course not. Why should I?'

'Because I don't trust anyone either. But mainly because I will feel less of a Charlie if we are both - exposed.' Lance looked determined.

Christophe shrugged in resigned acquiescence spread his hands, then insisted, 'And no companions.'

'Not even little me?' asked Caroline sweetly. A no and a non mingled emphatically.

'You don't look happy,' said Caroline looking at Lance's glum face.

Lance glowered. 'My feelings at the moment exactly rhyme with this gentleman's name.' Caroline chuckled. Christophe looked puzzled.

'Lucky you're the same build. The clothes should fit.' Caroline said, trying to raise some enthusiasm for the venture in her reluctant husband.

This made Lance even more irascible. He grumbled and insisted he was the slimmer. He had no enthusiasm for the plan.

Back at the chalet Caroline kept trying to humour him out of his black mood. 'Is this what you would call a denouement?'

'The word denouement means getting unknotted.' Lance growled - not amused.

'And I gather you feel the reverse should happen to me.'

'Exactly. Look - you will drive me there and then disappear – right?'

'Wrong. I'll stay to see that he doesn't pull a fast one on you.'

'If Christophe sees you he'll not go through with it.'

'I'll stay hidden. You'll be very vulnerable.'

'You can say that again.'

'You can't risk a double cross at this stage. Even if he is on the level, I'll bet he has someone covering him - if that's not the wrong way of putting it.'

'You're enjoying this aren't you, Caroline. Well, I am not.'

'Forget all that. Just concentrate. We can't fall at the last hurdle. Are you going to do it? Or would you rather I did it?'

'All right. All right. I'll go. I suppose I must. I just feel sort of stupid. What will I do if he doesn't recognise me amongst all the other naked – '

'What do you want to do? Wear a carnation.'

'Very funny. Look if you insist on coming and are going to serve any purpose, bring this with you.' Lance went to the back of the wardrobe and took out the rifle.

The smile left Caroline's face. 'Where on earth did you get this?'

'Never mind that. They'll almost certainly have glasses on you and the sight of that gun will maybe put any nonsense out of their minds.'

'But I can't shoot.'

'They don't know that.'

So it transpired that Caroline lay on a sand dune with a rifle, which she could not use, endeavouring to make it visible but only when no-one nearby was looking, among large pine trees which each sent out roots like the tentacles of a demented octopus, writhing and twisting over the sand; at ground level, at ankle breaking level and occasionally rising to sit upon height. She half hid behind one of the latter.

It was late afternoon and the beach was not very crowded. Lance took off his clothes and, without turning, walked off with as much dignity as he could muster.

He had toyed with the idea of taking a beach ball to give himself something to do but Christophe had been adamant that there were to be no extras.

He strode off into the sun at exactly the agreed time.

Even swinging his arms seemed awkward. Soon Caroline saw, from a long way off, a naked male figure emerge from a wooded area and walk towards her husband. She could not be sure it was Christophe; a man who was very much what he wore. As Christophe had predicted none of the other sun worshippers gave them as much as a glance. The men marched towards each other, stumbling occasionally on the uneven sand. Caroline was to tell Lance later that she was reminded of High Noon, but that she visualised Gary Cooper as having somewhat slimmer buttocks.

When the men were a short distance apart Christophe pointed towards two sets of clothing, waving loosely on makeshift lines propped up on slim canes, some distance apart back in the direction he had come from. It was obvious from the movement made by the merest zephyr of a wind that no weapons could possibly be concealed in any of the garments. The men approached each other, stopped, and on the spur of the moment Lance thrust out his arm and they briefly shook hands. It occurred to Caroline that if the Frenchman had taken the initiative they might be kissing each other's cheeks right now. She giggled.

Christophe beckoned to Lance to select whichever of the clothes he wished, another apparent gesture of transparent good faith. She saw Lance then Christophe walk over and each gather a set of clothes and dress hurriedly. As they turned away from the shore line and shuffled towards a car Caroline checked it to be empty with the binoculars that she had brought along unbeknown to Lance.

'A confullfrontation,' she thought and laughed - but she worried as she drove back.

The two men did not speak as they sped up the mountain road. Lance reckoned they were on a track roughly parallel to the Olmacci road but not so far up the hillside. Christophe concentrated intently on the rough road, gripping tightly at the steering wheel and throwing the car around the corners in the manner of a man familiar with the road, the car and fast driving. Lance buttoned up the tunic which was sagging loosely, and smiled. He was the slimmer.

The car turned into the woods and bounced up a narrow track of earth and loose stones. The stones rattled on the underside of the car like machine gun bullets. Lance wondered again what the hell he was doing here. I think too quickly, he mused. Or not at all, he contradicted himself.

They skidded to a halt as they turned into a dark grey courtyard. The two story house, similar to those in Olmacci, was also dark grey. Not inviting. Christophe leapt from the car and bounded for the door. Thinking the Frenchman was making a break for it, Lance swung himself out of the car, glad the period of inaction was over and, feeling swashbuckling and reckless, chased after him, almost tripped and he had to slow down to hold up the alien trousers which had started to slip from his waist.

Christophe turned a key many times in the lock before he pushed the stout door open. Lance was right behind him as he entered the small dark hallway. The Frenchman went straight towards another door and again took some time to open it. He held the door open for Lance to enter. Lance pushed past him into a sparsely furnished room with a barred window. Christophe nodded to a low bed in the corner of the room.

'Your body.'

Lance looked at the shape under a dishevelled bundle of bedclothes and was glad Caroline was not with him.

CHAPTER TWENTY FOUR

Caroline was flattered when she was approached and asked by Jean Two to report on the progress they had made. It was the first time she had taken the initiative in making contact. When Caroline told her that Lance had gone off up the hills with Christophe, who they now, she reported, regarded as number one suspect she positively smiled.

'Like you, I do not trust that man.'

'Can I help in any way?' asked Caroline.

'I was hoping you would ask that. I think perhaps there is something you could do now. Put on your oldest clothes. Something less - colourful, and meet me back here in a few minutes time. I would have preferred not to involve you but you seem to have done that yourself. But this is now serious. Do as I say, without question. Our reinforcements are at hand.'

Now excited, Caroline hurried off and did as she was asked. She did not put on her older clothes, she did not have any such with her, but something a little more subdued; a light brown jump suit and matching beret; if there were going to be action, she wanted to look her best. I can only work well if I look well, she persuaded herself. Jean Two was waiting impatiently for her at the wheel of her car and they immediately sped off towards the shore.

'What do you know of this man, Christophe?' asked Jean Two as the car lurched along the road.

'Very little. We think he may have murdered your colleague - we think so, but we do not know for sure. What do you think?'

'As I told you I have not had time to pursue that. That will be attended to later. She really does not matter at the moment. We cannot bring her back so we must finish the job she came to do.'

'Guns?'

Caroline thought the car was going to turn over.

'Guns,' exploded Jean Two angrily. 'What makes you say that?'

Caroline did not answer.

'You should not know. No-one should know. This operation leaks like a sieve.'

'I do not know. We guessed it must be guns or drugs. Not too difficult.' Caroline decided not to say any more as she feared that the, up to now, appreciative Jean Two was beginning to realise and resent the degree of their involvement.

Seeing the grim, determined, but slightly apprehensive expression Caroline wished that Lance was with her.

CHAPTER THIRTY TWO

Lance looked aghast at the heaped bedclothes. He stared at the pitiful bundle and noticed the wisps of red hair straggling up onto the crumpled pillow. His hands formed into claws as he turned on Christophe and advanced towards him. The Frenchman neatly side stepped and jumped over to the bedside and to Lance's horror he thumped the body. Lance leapt at Christophe in fury, his hand raised to strike the Frenchman.

Then in front of Lance's ever widening eyes the bedclothes stirred and a full shock of red hair emerged.

'Jean,' shouted Christophe, parrying the now wavering Lance. 'Wake up, we have a visitor.'

The gleaming hair shook and Jean head's appeared. She blinked and looked around. She looked sullen and did not speak.

'Say hullo to the white knight. He's come to identify the body.'

Lance collapsed into a chair, mesmerised.

'So you see that I did not kill her. Proof positive. Will you now go and destroy that silly letter? Now. I have no time to mess with the police.'

'I think,' Lance began shakily, 'I will want to know a little more before that, and confirmation from - Jean.'

Christophe looked at Lance and then at Jean. 'Right. I will explain briefly. Very briefly. I must go soon - now'. He looked at his wrist for the watch which wasn't there then at a clock with an angry gesture of impatience. 'I kidnapped her to save her from a murder trap I had pre knowledge of. I thought she was too lovely to kill.' He smiled at Jean. Jean did not smile. He continued. 'I drugged her. It was a rushed job. I am no expert. Jean was quite ill for some days. I feared that I might indeed have killed her. That I would have greatly regretted.'

'But the blood on the handkerchief?'

Christophe opened a drawer and produced a hypodermic. 'This. I put the handkerchief where I knew that her contact would see it. I gather that she passed on the right information. Smart girl.' He turned to Jean who was staring at the needle. 'Sorry, I took as little as was necessary.'

Jean turned away angrily.

'But why?' asked Lance.

'I did not want a search for her. It is not a big island. I might have become implicated. I knew the British police would put her right out of their minds as soon they were sure she was dead. She would be no further use to them then.'

'But why is she still captive?'

'Because this job is being done the French way. When I realised how nice a person she is - too nice - I feared she would botch up our plan. This is a vital case - no - a vital battle.'

'Which would have been won by now if you had not interfered.' Jean interrupted fiercely.

'Not with finality. You wear what you say - the kid gloves. We wish to end this. End it.' Christophe drew a hand across his throat. 'But I did not think you would get a reserve in place so soon - not the British. An interfering reserve.'

'Is this all to do with the guns?'

Jean and Christophe both looked surprised and listened intently as Lance told them of his exploit with Raoul at the old barn.

'How did you get mixed up in this?' asked Jean.

Lance did not admit that he too had thought she was too lovely to kill. 'I was looking forward to our tennis match. I wondered why you had vanished. The lady vanishes, that's it. Always had a fascination. Since the film, maybe.'

The other two looked at him in amazement.

'And one thing led to another.' Lance finished lamely.

'How is Judy doing?' asked Jean.

'She seems a very competent lady. We haven't seen much of her lately.'

Jean turned to Christophe. 'They have not tried to kill her also?'

'I don't know. They may not know who she is. She doesn't exactly look like you. They may be confused. I hope so. She is smart. Always does the unexpected.'

'Smarter than I was,' Jean complained ruefully.

She swung her legs out of the bed. She was fully clothed in light summer trousers and blouse, all somewhat rumpled.

'Has he - this man harmed you in any way?' Lance felt his role as rescuing hero slipping away.

'Not at all. He has looked after me very well. Given me everything I have wanted - and offered me more than I wanted, I may say.'

Christophe smiled in a self deprecating way and shrugged. 'I try to please.'

'Well, before we dash off mix me a drink like a good boy,' pleaded Jean with a trace of a smile. 'I feel rotten.'

As the Frenchman reached into a cupboard Lance noticed a neat plateful of tit bits obviously taken from the buffet. Christophe then took out two bottles and a glass, poured an orange juice - and Lance, although beginning to feel inured to surprises, gaped as he saw Christophe tip some Campari into it.

Jean gulped the concoction then, seeing Lance's bewildered expression, said with a shrug, 'Unusual, I know but it's got a real tang to it. I like it.'

'Thank God you do,' thought Lance, 'Or I might not be here.'

Out loud he said, 'Tang enough to hide the taste of a drug.'

Christophe nodded.

And the clue which helped lead me to this - the solution to a murder which never happened, thought Lance. Then still thinking of clues and murder he told them in detail of the possible extra body in the crypt, the disturbed trail in the maquis, the burnt straw, the breached fence and the blood stains. Jean looked worried but Christophe was less concerned.

He offered Lance a glass of the mixture which he declined.

'A death or two is almost inevitable in this activity - not important. We are after big people. The end justifies - as you English say.'

'Listen,' Lance interrupted firmly, 'I came here to find out if you murdered Jean. OK, you didn't. But I still know nothing of who you are or what you are - nothing. You saved Jean, but in spite of your big talk you seem to be a villain none the less. If so, I will let the letter lie and the police can find out what I know and work out what you're really up to.'

'No, don't do that.' It was Jean who spoke. 'I will never forgive this idiot for interfering in my work but he is on our side. He is a French Customs Officer. They have eccentric ways of working.'

'I am thought by the smugglers to be a local small time crook and source of valuable information.' explained Christophe. 'I informed the villians, as you call them, by a prearranged signal at the cafe when Jean was due to arrived and which chalet she had been allocated. I did this in order to gain their confidence. They said they wanted to establish her identity only so that they could keep clear of her and keep tabs on her activities. I was happy to minimize the British input. I didn't realise then that they planned to kill her. Which, you must agree would also have interfered with her work. They must have realized she would interfere too much. As soon as I learnt of there intentions I did what I did.'

'And at the cafe I thought you were just a lecherous creep. Which of course you are.'

Christophe shrugged.

'So he landed my back-up with the difficult job which I was specially prepared and trained for.'

'And which she seems to be doing very well.'

Jean grimaced.

'How the hell do you identify each other? Everyone is pretending to be someone else. How can you trust each other? How can I believe either of you?'

Jean removed a small credit card from her trouser pocket and showed him it. It was an unexceptional card made out in the name of a departmental store.

'A store which does not exist.'

Lance stared at it. He reached out and Jean relinquished it to him.

'We couldn't have anything that looked official.'

'Who else has one?' asked Lance.

'Only my contact Judy and this - creature.'

Christophe broke the silence. 'Today was the first time I have identified myself to Judy with the card and she to me. We exchanged notes on progress, not the full story of course, and I explained our meeting and told her that if you get up to any fancy tricks with me, she had to get hold of Caroline. She is tougher than Jean and she knows that we must not have the local police involved at this time. Just another insurance policy. So you had better destroy your letter. I am sure Caroline will not be harmed - but are you? This operation is desperately important. Nothing will be allowed to stand in its way.'

Seeing Lance's angry face he added, 'But you have no tricks in mind. Have you? So, it's all right.'

Lance could not think what to say.

'Where is your card now?' asked Jean turning to Christophe.

'In my clothes back at the chalet. As agreed I have absolutely nothing in these clothes.'

'I should hope not.' Lance glowered.

Jean looked at him. 'Why are you dressed like that. You both look ridiculous. It makes it difficult to take all this seriously.'

Lance looked sheepish as he searched about for something to enhance his appearance and effectiveness meanwhile explaining the reason for the ill fitting clothes. Jean laughed.

Lance found a brightly colourd tie which, brushing aside Christophe's protest, he bound round his trouser waist, and he abandoned the floppy tunic in favour of an old pullover.

He looked at Jean who now looked the smartest of the three. Her hair looked glorious. 'Beautiful.' He directed his stare at the copper tresses.

'It should be,' explained Jean. 'I have brushed this hair for hours on end. Nothing else to do.' She glared at Christophe.

Lance now spoke firmly to re-establish some vestige of authority. 'There is no doubt in my mind that there was an extra body in that coffin or someone went to extraordinary lengths to make it look as if that were so. We thought at one time that Judy might have gone to get your body out of the coffin to give you a decent burial. She doesn't say much.' complained Lance. 'We really never know what she's up to.'

'I should hope not.' Jean was thoughtful. 'Perhaps Judy had to kill someone. Someone who got in her way, or made an attempt on her life. It must have been that. I should have been there.'

Tears of anger and frustration welled up in her eyes. Again she glared at Christophe.

The Frenchman suddenly looked at the clock again and became agitated. 'Mon Dieu, I must leave you. I have urgent business to attend to. I will have to lock you up again. Both of you. I'll be back soon.' He took the keys out of his pocket.

'You're going nowhere without me,' insisted Jean.

'Nor me,' added Lance.

Christophe moved towards an inner door but the other two blocked his way.

'If your appointment is so urgent you don't have time to struggle with us.'

Jean adopted a karate type stance. Lance, seeing her aggressive pose, put up his hands like an old time boxer.

Christophe hand shot across his chest to where his gun would normally be hidden, shook his head in exasperation and looked the clock again.

Lance smiled triumphantly. 'And the letter to the police must be destroyed - by me.'

Christophe yielded with an exasperated sigh. 'Right, if you must come you can make yourself useful. I won't now have time to collect my assistant.'

He reached into a cupboard and for the second time in two days Lance had a rifle thrust into his hands.

CHAPTER TWENTY SIX

In the darkness of the moonless evening two shadowy figures poured some fluid over a large heap of stacked wood. They stood well back then tossed blazing brands onto the pile. They then ran for fifty metres over the flat ground and repeated the performance. Against the light of the now blazing fires the shadows turned to silhouettes which now slunk away across the wide flat area to the barn, scene of the recent shootout involving Lance and Raoul. The now familiar noise of the motor bikes started to roar around them in a deafening swirl, blanketing out all other sounds.

When the fire raisers were far enough away Christophe growled 'Just do it.' left them and scrambled off up the mountain side. Thus instructed Jean and Lance hurried towards the flames, stopped, lay down, and waited in the flickering shadows looking towards the hills in the direction Christophe had taken. The constant noise was literally deafening which was disconcerting as they realised that they could not have heard an army tank if it had crept up on them. They could only wait. Then after what seemed an eternity they saw, high up the steep hillside, a small flame flicker, then a few minutes later another one fifty metres away. The two fires suddenly flared and lit up the trees and rocks around them. They were the same distance apart as the fires on the flat ground.

Christophe had done his part. This was their signal. Lance and Jean scurried forward, each carrying a heavy fire extinguisher. They separated and each directed the chemical jet at one of the fires lit minutes earlier by the shadowy figures. It was apparent that a lot of petrol had been thrown on the timber as the flames took some time to douse. As they laboured they lay down as flat as they could to avoid being seen by the rapidly departing couple who had set off these first fires. The retreating pair had their backs to the fire fighters as they hurried towards the barn.

It was awkward work but they kept the foam spewing on the dying embers until the fires were darkened then threw the, still squirting, extinguishers on the fires and ran for the nearest clump of bushes.

The departing figures of the two original fire raisers had almost reached the barn before they turned, saw what was happening, put there heads together for a moment then picked up more petrol canisters and rushed back towards the damped out fires. Someone in the barn shot wildly past the fires in an attempt to cover the fire raisers. Lance cocked his rifle, took careful aim and his single shot passed near enough to hit one of the canisters being carried by the fire raisers and it instantly burst into flames. The two shadowy figures turned and fled back to the barn; one of them slapping out the flames coming from burning trousers. Lance sent another couple of shots after the rapidly retreating pair causing them to go faster and jink from side to side.

All was quiet for a long time as none of the protagonists could decide what to do next. Then a roar, greater even than the sound of the bikes, swept in a wave towards them. It increased in volume quickly - then it was above them. The bikes in turn became louder as if in answer. Lance could now make out a large black mass speeding across the sky immediately above him and heard the spluttering of an engine being throttled back. Moments later the sky was filled with light. This was followed by a horrendous crashing noise contained and amplified by the surrounding mountains. The sky went dark for a split second. Then a huge ball of fire erupted from the hillside halfway between the fires so recently lit up there by Christophe. The sound was now the crackling of dry trees bursting into flame. If anyone screamed, no one heard. The flames started to trickle down the hillside like a luminous stream. An occasional secondary explosion rent the air. The motor cycle sound faded quickly as if the cyclists had decided to free wheel down and away. Soon all was silent again and Lance and Jean scrambled back to the car, picking up Christophe as they fled from the scene.

'There were guns in that plane?' asked Lance when they returned to the silence of the car.

'Yes,' replied Christophe. He then turned to Jean. 'And a big man.'

'Who we had hoped to capture.'

'And who would have passed the buck to the small men and been protected by businessmen - and your politicians.'

'And yours.'

'I don't understand.' Lance protested.

'You don't need to understand,' said Jean. 'Enough to know that guns enough to kill many thousands of people have been destroyed'

'So, some munitions factory goes on overtime.'

'This has been a complex operation. It will not be easily set up again. Some of the guilty have also been destroyed.'

'And an innocent.'

'What do you mean?'

'As you are alive. Who was in the coffin?' Lance turned to Christophe. 'Or did you fake all that? Like your blood sample.'

'Not me. I had enough to do.'

'All our team seems to be present and correct - which reminds me we must contact Judy' said Jean.

'We have lost no-one either so that, as you say, is that.' Christophe also looked pleased.

'We must tell Judy what has happened. She will be angry to have missed the action.'

Jean looked happy for the first time since Lance had found her; pleased with her belated involvement.

Lance cut into their contentment. 'So whose was the body? I can't believe anyone would have troubled with such an elaborate deception. I just can't believe it.'

Both the others shrugged without too much display of concern.

'We might find out some day,' said Christophe off handedly.

Jean nodded, then eagerly. 'So, let's find Judy now. She must be quite a girl. I'm looking forward to meeting her.'

'What do you mean? Haven't you met her before?'

'No. Never. I think she's spent a lot of time out here.'

Lance looked unbelieving, then exploded. 'Good God.'

Lance pushed Christophe roughly aside, as he was about to enter the car, scrambled into the driving seat and took over. The Frenchman had to jump to it to get into the car again.

The car leapt forward. Lance had never driven so fast in his life.

CHAPTER TWENTY SEVEN

'Raoul is behind this I'm now certain. That shot must have been him. He's a marksman. I think I know where he'll make for now. Let's go,' shouted Jean Two. She sounded furious.

'He certainly knew where the guns were,' affirmed Caroline.

Jean Two turned the car downhill and headed towards the harbour. Caroline could see coloured lights and many more boats than normal. I was right, she thought. They'll use Saint Erasmus as cover. She looked at the tense but determined face at the wheel beside her and she knew she was in good hands.

When they reached the shore Jean hurried to a small jetty and jumped into a tiny motor boat. Bernard the bus driver was already sitting at the wheel. Caroline scrambled in. Bernard turned a key and they powered out to sea, wending a way between the numerous brightly festooned craft. They hove to alongside a modest motor yacht with the name 'Villamaquis sur la Mer'.

'Does this belong to the sisters?'

'It does but they never use it now. But someone does and that someone is our target. The crooks are planning their getaway on this yacht. I know that. If we can surprise them we can send for the police while we hold them. So, not a sound.'

They stayed on the small boat for a few minutes listening carefully. They could hear the indistinct sound of voices. Someone was aboard. Caroline shivered. Bernard pulled their boat slowly along to the point where a short rope ladder hung over the side. Jean Two leant over and cut loose a small rowing boat tied to the yacht, pushed it to drift away, then climbed up gingerly and lay flat on the deck of the yacht and listened, then she signalled for the others to follow. They climbed, as quietly as they could, on to the unlit deck. They stopped and listened again and Caroline heard a faint laugh. Jean Two turned to Bernard and whispered that he should wait on deck and keep watch. She then crept up to the doorway, kicked the door open ferociously, leapt into the cabin and hit the light switch.

'Keep still,' she shouted. 'One word or movement and you're dead.' She had a hand gun directed at the backs of the sitting couple. They were motionless. As soon as Caroline had pressed herself into the small cabin she saw that the tense figures were those of Raoul and Rhoda. She felt a pang of disappointment.

'Get some rope. Four pieces,' barked Jean Two.

Caroline had no difficulty in finding pieces of rope and cord of all thicknesses. Guessing what it was wanted for, she picked four suitable lengths.

'Tie them or hold this gun.'

Caroline looked at the gun and said. 'I'll tie them.'

Reluctantly she proceeded to do so. She bound their hands tightly behind their backs. She recalled Raoul's ability to bend steel bars. As she moved round to tie their ankles she averted her eyes. Jean Two took pieces of rough insulating tape and stuck it over the mouths of the trussed pair. Caroline checked that their nostrils were unblocked. Jean Two snorted and carefully checked that the prisoners were securely tied. She jerked Raoul's bonds tighter.

When this was all done she returned the gun to her pocket and turned to Caroline. 'Can you handle a motor boat?'

'No. And certainly not with so many other boats about.'

'I can't either. I'll take Bernard and send him straight back to help you while I go get the police. The motor boat is too small to take us all and this boat has not sailed for years. You guard this pair until we get back. Watch for tricks. They're a devious and dangerous pair. I'll go now. Be back soon. I'll go and tell Bernard to make sure the boat is immobilised as an extra precaution.'

Caroline was feeling her mouth go very dry with the tension so she reached for a grape from a bowl on the table and crushed the sweet fruit in her mouth. She was reassured to see Jean Two also reach, with slightly shaking hands, for some of the grapes and chew them fiercely, nervously spitting the pips on to the floor. She reached for her gun and handed it to Caroline. Jean Two was gone for a few minutes then returned grim faced, touched the barrel of the revolver in Caroline's hand so that it pointed straight at the back of Raoul's head.

'Keep it just there.'

She then took a last look round and went off up the stairway.

The anxious Caroline, feeling the weight of the gun in her hand, wondered if she really could use it. She had vague recollections that there was a safety catch and realized she didn't know where. She shouted, 'Judy.' There was no response. After a few moments the small boat puttered away and all was quiet. Caroline suddenly felt very lonely and completely bewildered.

CHAPTER TWENTY EIGHT

Lance hurtled the car down the hill. The two normally tough law enforcers crouched quaking in their seats; squeaking the occasional protest. He was gripping the wheel so tightly his hands were hurting. He was determined to get to Caroline as quickly as possible and he knew that meant staying on the road. The band at the Villamaquis was playing full blast although most of the holiday makers were down at the Harbour. He drove across the grass and stopped as near as he could to the chalet and bounded up to it. It was in darkness. He turned the switch and looked around. A piece of paper lay on the table. A message in Caroline's hand.

It read: 'Have gone with Jean to the boat "Villamaquis sur la Mer" just outside harbour, come quickly. We are closing in. Use motor boat in harbour - berth 37. Herewith keys. Bring Christophe if he is with you. He is one of us.' A set of keys lay by the message.

Lance bumped into Christophe as he rushed back to the car. 'Quick. to the harbour.'

Christophe screamed, 'The letter.'

Lance hesitated for a moment then tore across the grass and ripped an envelope from under the wastepaper bin.

He sprinted to the car. Christophe followed. They careered down the hill on the shortest route to the sea.

'She's quite a girl, this Judy,' shouted Christophe.

Jean could only nod her head. They screamed on to the harbour to the smell of burning brakes and tyres, causing some sailors dancing in celebration of their guardian saint to call urgently for his help. Lance drove right along the edge of the harbour looking at the berth numbers. He braked violently at berth thirty seven. A small motor boat lay there.

Christophe took one look at it and shouted, 'Forget that toy. I'll get a real boat.' Christophe rushed to a brightly coloured office nearby. He came out half hauling a uniformed man. Christophe was obviously recognised. They were led down to a large, powerful customs boat. The engine sprung into life almost as soon as they were aboard. As Lance was telling them where he wanted to go the bow rose out of the water and they soared out of the harbour. The man at the wheel knew the boat they were seeking. Lance had been dreading the search for it. It was a dark night but every boat and ship for miles was dressed overall and sparkling with lights of all colours. The fast launch slalomed its way amongst the festive craft. Exuberant and intoxicated crews cheered their passing. They had not gone far into the slightly less calm water when they heard a deep roar, then a huge flash lit up the water and pieces of a boat soared into the air. A small fragment hit the deck. Lance let out a sob.

'The light,' shouted Christophe.

A searchlight on the boat immediately flashed on and swept across the surface of the sea. They sped towards the doomed vessel. As they approached they had to slow down, as the pieces of flotsam were now larger. They circled the area; their powerful beam lighting up the scene of the disaster. They could see nothing but floating timber and plastic. The water was still boiling in the middle of the wrack. Soon an unpleasant slick of oil was flattening the brisk little waves, adding to the air of desolation. They spent some time picking their way through the debris. Then they found three brightly coloured lifebelts floating together - all empty.

Lance was now leaning over the side peering desperately for any hopeful sign. Several times he had to be restrained from diving in. Forlornly they circled wider and wider searching, in particular, between the wreckage and the shore where any survivor would surely have headed.

Then they spied what they were looking for - but dreaded finding. An air filled ballooned jacket was keeping a body afloat. Slowly the boat was brought alongside and a crew member jumped in while another leant over with a boat hook. Lance pushed him aside and took the hook and engaged it gently at the collar. He pulled carefully as the man in the sea pushed up. The others bent over and helped. The body was laid gently on the deck.

As it was carefully turned over, Lance closed his eyes. He took a deep breath, opened them and looked. The features were badly mutilated but just recognisable.

The large moustache made it easy. It was Bernard, the bus driver. The skin was badly discoloured and now the moustache was the only real looking part of the face. There was no glimmer of life in the limp body.

The slowness of the boat now drove Lance to distraction. He wanted to race over the water covering every inch in the least possible time. He also wanted them to be as careful as possible.

They were now circling some way from the boat.

There was little debris here and no oil. They were heading out to sea on a wide sweep and Lance was desperately impatient for them to get back round between the boat and the shore again and was saying so emphatically when the light caught a small dark blob on the surface. The beam was moved a little and illuminated two more similar objects close by the first sighting. As they drew nearer they detected faint splashing. They sailed cautiously closer and saw three heads close together.

CHAPTER TWENTY NINE

Bursting with frustration after days of inactivity Jean jumped into the sea and helped push the swimmers up to the hands stretching down from the boat. When Caroline, Raoul and Rhoda were safely in the boat and they were heading slowly back to the harbour, Christophe asked gruffly. 'Why the hell were you heading out to sea? And why no lifebelts.'

Caroline spluttered and spat. 'There was a yacht just thirty yards away beyond us. We tried to get to it. It didn't see us.' She choked, then went on. 'It sailed off just as we were getting to it. To get away. It was raining bits of boat then. And there were no lifejackets. Someone must have thrown them overboard.'

Lance reached out his hand. 'Thank you Raoul. You are a wonderful man. That must have been quite a swim with two ladies to haul along.'

Raoul did not take the proffered hand and looked sheepish as the girls laughed. 'I cannot swim. I am a mountain man. It was the ladies who kept me afloat. They are the wonderful ones.' He squeezed Rhoda's hand and nodded appreciatively to Caroline.

Lance looked at Caroline. 'When did you realise?'

'I was covering the supposed villains with a gun and I didn't know if the safety catch was on or off or even where it was so I shouted Judy, but she didn't respond. Not a flicker. It wasn't her name. She would have reacted if it had been. I know she would. No one was supposed to know it. Then it flashed into my mind that she had spat out her grape seeds. I remembered the seeds in the coffin. I panicked and went to the port hole and saw she was alone in the boat - driving it away. I shouted to Bernard. No reply. So I went up. There he was. Lying. A knife in his back. So I released our friends as quickly as I could and we jumped into the sea and swam for the boat nearby without a moment's hesitation. We realised something nasty was going to happen. As soon as everything blew up, the boat we were heading for sailed away.' She paused and drew a deep breath. 'And you? You must have got my message. What brought you down to the villas in the proverbial nick of time?'

'When the real Jean here said she had never met Judy. I remember Jean Two saying that Jean had lovely skin. Jean here, as you can see, has one really conspicuous feature. Anyone describing her would mention the hair. I should have picked that up at the time. Anyway, I realised she must have been talking about the fair skin of the woman she thought was Jean Faulds when she murdered her.'

Jean's head sunk in her hands. 'So Judy it was who died.' Everyone was silent for a few moments.

Christophe thumped the table angrily and let out a groan. He reached out a hand to comfort Jean but withdrew it. His faced twisted as he thought of his part in Judy's death. 'I almost had her. Jean Two – whoever she is. I traced their headquarters to Olmacci. But before I could get to it, they had blown it up. A lot of good evidence gone. Killed one of their own people. Obviously of no importance. Someone tipped them off or frightened them. Americans up there I heard.' Caroline allowed herself a small grimace. Christophe continued, 'What the hell for I don't know. Of course I didn't know Jean Two, as you call her, was one of the villains then. She fooled me.'

Lance and Caroline exchanged sheepish glances.

Christophe added, 'But of course if I had got her then, we would not have brought down this plane load and the big man aboard.'

Caroline intervened thoughtfully.

'So Jean two, I don't suppose we will ever know her real name, will have wiped up the blood when she realized the crypt was getting visitors. It could have contradicted her blood stained hankerchief.'

'And moved the body.' added Lance then shook his head in dismay as he noticed that Caroline's trouser leg was burnt. 'How did you get burnt if you left the boat before the explosion?'

'An idiot shot at me when I had a can of petrol in my hand.'

Lance looked at Christophe and whispered. 'I never shoot to kill. Just can't.'

Christophe smiled. 'Bon chance.'

Caroline heard, understood and snorted. 'Friendly fire.'

She put her hand down to the burnt patch and pulled the cloth over to hide the scorched flesh. She winced and was about to say something when she noticed Bernard's body and gasped.

'It's him. That man whose death saved our lives. Why?'

'She must have killed him so that he couldn't talk. Just tidying up.' Jean spoke quietly as the others looked at the body of the man who would never talk again.

'The case,' screamed Rhoda. 'Where is his case?'

The others looked at her as if she were mad.

'He had a case always chained to his wrist.'

Someone turned over the body with his foot. The left hand was missing only a raw stump left.

'We must find his case. Please. Please.'

A crew member heard this and shouted across. 'There was a black box thing floating not far from the body.'

'Find it, please,' pleaded Rhoda.

Seeing the desperation in her face, they circled back to where the body had been taken from the water and soon found the brief case floating on the oily water, a bloody, severed hand still attached to it.

The customs officer examined it. 'That's a self destruct case. We come across them quite a lot. He didn't want anyone to get at what was in it. If anyone not knowing the code had opened it, the contents would have been incinerated.'

Rhoda looked at it. 'That's right. It has - papers in it that Mona was desp - was anxious to get back from him. Even Raoul couldn't get it. We knew Bernard just had to press the button, which he would have done if Raoul had attacked him. It was his defence as well as his threat.'

Rhoda explained that Mona had been charged with a particularly nasty crime which she could not disprove. She had been teaching at a school when a singularly unpleasant child who she had reprimanded had accused her of foul abuses. The parents were powerful and influential and also unpleasant. They convinced the police and the press. Mona is not very tactful. She antagonised them. She was just a young, penniless teacher. She thought she did not have a chance and that anyway her name was besmirched beyond remedy, so she had jumped bail and fled to Corsica, changed her name, got a job with a tour company, met and befriended Rhoda and they had lived thereafter as sisters. They set up their own company. Bernard, then a trusted employee, had been sent by the sisters to collect a deathbed confession from the child now grown up and dying of a painful illness and with a guilty conscience. This would have cleared Mona, but instead Bernard had used it to blackmail Mona into letting the gun runners use Villamaquis as cover for their activities. This was to have been the last run, then Mona would have been given the papers.

Mona had believed this promise. Rhoda had not. Even when Raoul had told the sisters of the guns in the barn Mona would not agree to use that information to pressure the blackmailers.

The customs officer took charge of the case and indicated that he could get to the contents.

'Just like bomb disposal,' he said.

As they stood silent, a boatman hooked in from the surface of the sea a bright yellow anorak which Caroline confirmed was the one Jean Two had been wearing.

'To make us think she went down with the boat. So that we would not search for her. She's thought of everything.' There was a note of respect in Christophe's voice. He turned to the radio operator and set up a sea, land and air search for the fleeing killer. 'She'll be the only boat moving tonight. We'll soon pick her up. Particularily if she doesn't think we'll be looking for her.'

Caroline looked puzzled, 'What was she thinking about when she asked me to leave a message to you to come to the boat?'

No one could answer that. 'Maybe to reinforce the idea that she was genuine,' ventured Lance.

Christophe added, 'That's right; and I'm sure she thought that she had things set up so that you were going to be too late anyway.'

The answer to their last question about the message was provided the following day when the boat at berth thirty seven was found to have an explosive charge set to go off one minute after the engine started.
This was further explanation why Jean Two had sailed away so confidently; and was caught so easily.

When that boat was searched the pathetic remains of Judy's much moved body was found. In a last move, it was flown back to Britain for a small, quiet, family funeral.

Raoul turned to Rhoda and quietly asked. 'Who is this Jean Two they are they talking about?'

Rhoda whispered back. 'The woman who held the gun at the back of our heads. Jean Faulds she called herself. She stayed at the Villas. Chalet eight. You may have seen something of her about the place.'

'Seen something of her,' grinned Raoul. 'I've seen all of her. She appeared on the hillside naked and disrupted things when I was waiting for grandfather's funeral. Caused chaos among the pall bearers. I had to help them up the hill. Pity granpere missed it. He would have enjoyed that.'

Caroline whispered to Lance. 'Another mystery solved. A diversion while they put the other body in the coffin. Resourceful lass.'

Seeing that Rhoda wasn't looking too pleased Raoul stopped smiling and put his arm round her waist his huge hand cupping an appropriately proportioned bosom. 'She didn't have a body like yours.'

Rhoda smiled but said grimly. 'What a tragedy this has all been.'

Raoul also looked sober, 'Perhaps if you consented to a request that you become Mrs Fournier, and do so on a boat on Saint Erasmus day, the good saint will look after us from now on.'

Rhoda beamed, turned to Raoul and nodded vigorously.

Raoul now turned to the others. 'We have done our courting on this boat since the fire in the old storehouse. So this is the right place as well as the right time for us.' He grinned happily..

The big man hugged Rhoda fiercely and Lance noticed that her cheek was now grazed again.

Lance and Caroline exchanged knowing glances. They all competed in telling their parts of the story, even Christophe joined in the excited and mainly frank discussion but Lance and Caroline never told Raoul of the use that had been made of his grandfather's coffin. Nor the sisters where their missing sheet was now.

'Right where to now.' asked the boat captain.

'To the nearest big hot dry towel.' replied Caroline emphatically.

'And a doctor.' added Christophe who had noticed the scorched leg.

Back home when Caroline was unpacking she came across the Champagne bottle neck. She looked at it quietly then said to Lance. 'We reached the Champagne with the cork still intact.'

She laid it on the mantelpiece. 'Whenever I look at that, I will think of Jean.'

Lance nodded slowly and with a catch in his voice murmured, 'And if I ever drink Champagne again, I will drink a toast to Judy. The girl who didn't matter. The girl who was not too lovely to kill.'

THE END